Neptune Rising

Rod Gillies

Also by Rod Gillies

Red Mercury

Copyright 2013 Rod Gillies

All rights reserved

ISBN-10: 1484981111   ISBN-13: 978-1484981115

For everyone who likes a bit of clank (or pirates)

Windward Passage, off Hispaniola

The boy clutched the stern rail and stared back at the ships. He blinked, determined not to cry – not in front of these last remaining members of the crew.

On his father's orders he had been dragged unceremoniously from the bridge – out of the wheelhouse, down into the depths of the vessel, through companionways packed tight with grim-faced men preparing for battle.

Ignoring his protests and ineffective blows, the sailors had bundled him into the launch. The lines were cast off and the boat steamed away, fire box stoked to bursting, paddles thrashing at the water, seeking safety in the gathering night.

Smoke and fire erupted from a dozen broad muzzles, followed a split-second later by the booming concussion. Distracted from his anger by the spectacle, the boy thrilled at the power and noise of the cannon, imagining the incendiary shells ripping an arc through the sky towards his father's enemies.

The reply, when it came, crushed his excitement. The full immensity of the English dreadnought became suddenly apparent as the thunder flash of her broadside rippled down her length. Three times the size of his father's vessel, carrying four times the guns, the warship was massive. More, she was possessed of all the fearsome efficiency the Royal Navy instilled in its men.

One relentless fusillade followed another, the dreadnought's gunners quickly finding the range, rounds thumping into the target with a merciless accuracy. At first there were scattered shots in response, but these faded away as flames blossomed on board. As the English shells rained down, the ship the boy had called home was reduced to a slowly-sinking bonfire.

He watched the one-sided battle recede in the launch's wake, resisting the urge to look away until long after the fire's orange glow had been extinguished. Not old enough to fight, but old enough to want to, Jack Rackham burned with shame as he sailed away into the darkness.

Ypres

The star shell burst over No Man's Land and began its descent, a phosphorous glare painting the landscape in stark flickers of white.

The crawling men pushed themselves into the mud. All veterans of the trenches, they buried their faces in the crooks of their arms, attempting to stop tell-tale clouds of breath forming in the cold air – a tactic learned from bitter lessons handed out by German snipers.

Jones found it ironic the weapons that scared him most were not the giant war machines that stalked the trench-scarred battlefields – you could see them coming. What brought him out in a clammy sweat was the thought of his face coming into focus in the telescopic sight on some Mauser rifle. You'd never know. Might not even hear the shot. Although granted, it would at least be mercifully swift.

No shots came this time though, and as the star shell spluttered out its last light, Jones and his men were plunged back into darkness and relative safety. He lay in the sucking cold of the mud, waiting for his eyes to adjust. Eventually able to distinguish his surroundings, even if only in shades of darkest grey, he waved the men forward.

After an exhausting hour slithering on their bellies, punctuated by frozen moments of phosphor-lit fear, the four men reached their destination. The ruined observation post was long-since abandoned, the collapsed trenches it had served relegated to No Man's Land months before as the front line shifted back and forth.

Jones wasn't sure which side had built the shelter in the first place. Not that it mattered. Any port in a storm and all that. The soldiers squeezed into the cramped confines of the squat building, glad to be out of the quagmire.

"Not long now boys," said Jones. "We'll wait for daylight, then in and out, and back for lunch."

His companions nodded, eyes wide in filthy faces. Carson, Wills and Sergeant Mackenzie had all volunteered for the mission. Jones wondered if they were regretting it now as the sick tension built up. He'd never ask of course, not the done thing. There were clear expectations of the officer class – a stiff upper lip and snappy one-liners in the face of danger. Never mind the exhausting nausea which affected him every bit as much as his men.

Jones rolled his aching shoulders and shifted, trying to get comfortable. He leaned his head back and regarded the lightening sky through the rotten timbers of the roof. The next thing he knew, he was snapping awake at a touch on his shoulder.

"Fritz is moving," whispered Mackenzie.

Jones flicked the clasp on his pocket watch and frowned down at the luminous dots around its face. He had dozed for twenty minutes.

"You looked like you needed the kip Major."

He gave the Scotsman a grateful nod and raised his head to peer through the observation slit. He could see nothing, but his ears picked up the rumble of engines and the tramp of feet. Mackenzie was right, somewhere out there an army was stirring.

As dawn broke, the German guns opened fire. The synchronised thunder followed long seconds later by the hollow crumps of explosions in the distance as the shells fell back to earth. After ten minutes of sustained fire, the artillery fell abruptly silent, its clamour replaced with the shouts of German officers and the noise of massed infantry on the move.

Jones couldn't help but feel a little sorry for the Germans as the first ghostly figures moved past them in the dim light. Even if the British hadn't already known about this particular assault, the artillery fire would have done little damage to the deeply-fortified positions, serving no purpose other than to warn the boys of the Queen's Guards the Hun was on his way. Why did the army chiefs on both sides still insist on throwing away the element of surprise like this? Conventional military wisdom, supposed Jones. Something his current mission had little to do with.

The press of troops heading for the British lines grew thicker. German riflemen led the advance, picking their way through the barbed wire and craters. Behind them came pairs of men managing the heavier weapons, one carrying a box of ammunition, the other struggling under the unwieldy burden of a Spandau machine gun and its tripod mounting. Once within range of the enemy, the fearsome gun would be braced into place, its hand-cranked mechanism capable of blasting out a hundred rounds in less than a minute.

Here and there across the battlefield, the infantry made space for the ugly box shapes of tanks. The riveted metal beasts rumbled alongside the men, growling out clouds of dirty smoke, the thick links of their treads cutting new ruts into the mud.

Behind the men and armoured vehicles lumbered the enormous frame of a four-legged walker. The articulated toe plates of its feet adjusted to the uneven terrain as it lurched past the concealed observers, shaking the ground, pistons expanding and contracting with each ponderous step. Atop the wide platform of the walker's deck, wreathed in wisps of expelled steam, figures scurried back and forth, preparing carbines and mortars to unleash a deadly hail of metal into the British trenches.

No regular soldier on either side envied the men who rode the walkers, despite their elevated position and heavy armaments. The steel monsters always drew fire in any battle – magnets for artillery and aerial bombardment, resulting in terrible casualties amongst the crews. The walkers were damned impressive in a parade, and Jones knew the top brass revelled in their mechanical power, but he had seen too many of the contraptions blown to shrapnel when a round punctured their huge boilers.

The dawn's light filtered through the clouds, and the full scale of the offensive became clear, Jones losing count as wave after wave of men and machinery rolled past his position. The Hun wasn't messing around here – this was a serious push.

Just as well it was no surprise. Poor old Fritz was in for a rough time. The Guards had been bracing for this particular assault for over a month now, thanks to the tipsy German officers who had ordered their schnapps from a waiter whose ears belonged to England.

The infiltrators lay concealed in the abandoned outpost until the last of the advancing troops filed past. As the first barks of gunfire echoed from the battle now being joined to the west, Jones stood, stretching the knots out of his muscles.

In the growing light he took in his men's appearance – all, like himself, dressed in German uniforms. Pulling the clothing from the enemy corpses scattered across No Man's Land had been one of the mission's more unpleasant preparatory tasks.

"Right chaps," he said, taking a bloodstained bandage from his pocket and tying it around his head. "The sooner we get this over and done with, the sooner we can get out of this ridiculous clobber."

*

Colonel Kramer turned from the map table as the wounded officer was helped into the command bunker. The man's uniform was filthy, as was the garb of the private who supported him.

Major Von Stalhein, Kramer's second-in-command, grimaced at the state of the new arrivals. Typical aristocrat, thought Kramer, more concerned with a bit of mud than the information the man apparently bore.

The injured soldier attempted a salute, swaying on his feet. Kramer pulled out a chair.

"Take a seat Captain. We have plenty to spare."

The wounded man sank gratefully into the canvas chair. He blinked, casting tired eyes around the bunker. "Where is everyone?" he asked.

"Every man who could be spared is at the front," snapped Von Stalhein.

"We have thrown everything into this offensive," said Kramer. "When the gas alarm sounded, I sent the others to the shelters. The Major here has been reduced to making his own coffee."

Von Stalhein scowled and Kramer allowed himself a smile. He did enjoy twisting the tail of his stuck-up subordinate. "Perhaps you could go and rustle up a mug for the Captain? He looks like he could do with it."

The Major stared back, clearly aghast at the suggestion. Kramer held his gaze until Von Stalhein offered a grudging salute and stomped from the room. Kramer returned his attention to the seated man.

"So my friend, what is this message that is so important?"

The soldier bent forward, fumbling in his leather pack. When he straightened, the dazed expression was gone, replaced with a grim determination. The hand came out of the bag holding a pistol.

"Queen Victoria sends her regards."

Kramer was stunned, as much at hearing English spoken within his command post as at the sudden appearance of the weapon. His faculties deserted him, his ability to think, to react, replaced with a lonely thought echoing round in his head: how could he have been taken in by such a simple deception? By the time he gathered his wits, he had already been disarmed by the man's companion.

The Englishman gave a weary smile and reached up to pull the bandage from his head.

He spoke to his compatriot. "Watch him."

Kramer stood seething as the imposter tucked away his weapon and began scouring the tables of the command post, moving methodically round the room, grabbing handfuls of papers and stuffing them into his bag. He paused before the wireless desk, contemplating the stacks of radio equipment, a baffling collection knobs and switches.

He reached out and lifted a wooden box, its front studded with dials. With a jerk, he pulled the cables from the device's rear and lifted it clear. Kramer winced. He had hoped the Englishman wouldn't grasp the box's significance. Whatever happened, he could not allow them to take the cipher machine. Kramer took a step forward.

The butt of the gun smashed between his shoulder blades and he crumpled to the floor in agony. The figure looming over him turned the carbine, bringing the muzzle back round to point into Kramer's face.

"Dinnae bother..." came the accented growl.

"Mackenzie," snapped the Englishman, distracted from his looting. "That's enough."

The soldier stepped back, frowning at the reprimand.

Kramer hauled himself to his feet, pain shooting across the muscles of his back. "There is no honour in this..." he said, finally finding his voice.

The man glared across the bunker. "You lost all honour when you dropped the gas shells, Colonel."

The words struck Kramer like a slap in the face. He had argued with High Command not to deploy the poison gas. It was a coward's weapon, and an ineffective one at that. But he had been overruled, his superiors desperate to break the deadlock of the trenches. Kramer had watched through his spyglass, appalled as the British soldiers suffocated. No enemy deserved such a death, the soft tissues of the throat burning in agony as the lungs collapsed.

"Your honour too is tainted," he said. "You deployed gas this very morning..."

The Englishman's expression switched from anger to amusement. He pulled a metal canteen from his pack and tossed it onto the map table, sending the carefully arranged formation markers tumbling.

"Only a little flask of the stuff. A whiff under your detector pipe, and you all went scuttling for cover. Like cockroaches."

Despite himself, Kramer was impressed with the ruse. "You came prepared."

"We had plenty of time to get ready. We've known about your offensive for some time." The Englishman smiled at Kramer's reaction, although the eyes remained cold. "The British lines are all set to give your men the appropriate reception."

Two soldiers burst into the command post and Kramer's heart lurched in hope, only to have it dashed as he spotted the slumped form they dragged between them. They dumped the body on the floor and made their report.

"Nobody around. All hiding from the gas," said the first man.

"But we found this one in the galley," said the other, gesturing to the corpse. "He picked a fight. He lost."

So Von Stalhein died with honour, thought Kramer. Perhaps he had underestimated the man after all.

The English officer listened to his men before returning his attention to Kramer. "Right then Colonel. Time to take a walk. You're coming with us."

Von Stalhein's body drew Kramer's eye. How ironic – the arrogant fool providing the honourable example. He drew his shoulders back and shook his head.

"I cannot allow you to kidnap me."

The Englishman stared at him, a measure of respect in his dark gaze. "We thought you might say that..."

He drew a curiously-shaped pistol, different to the one he had brandished earlier. He adjusted a dial mounted above the grip and a high-pitched whine began to emerge from the gun. The man's companions traded nervous looks and backed away as their leader raised the pistol.

Kramer mastered his nerves. Whatever this exotic weapon was, one death was very much like another. He pulled himself to attention, glaring at the man who had hoodwinked him.

"Get on with it."

The Englishman pulled the trigger.

*

The lightning's blue crackle faded away, leaving the soldiers blinking at the after-images dancing around their vision. Jones nudged the fallen German with his foot. Little curls of smoke rose from scorched patches on the man's uniform.

"Still alive?" asked Mackenzie.

"And sleeping soundly for the next six hours, if this contraption has done its job," said Jones. "Mind you, he'll wake up with a hangover that would kill a horse." He tucked the electrical pistol away and turned to Carson and Wills. "Go and find a stretcher. I'll be buggered if I'm lugging him all the way back by myself. Mackenzie, help me set the explosives."

The Sergeant fished into his pack and pulled out a string bag bulging with shiny black spheres. "Fifteen minutes?" he asked.

"Ten," said Jones. No point risking a stray guard stumbling on the scene. The whole point of the exercise was to leave the wreckage of the bunker safely on top of any evidence the command post had been ransacked and the Colonel kidnapped.

They turned the clockwork timers on each of the compact demolition charges, starting them ticking quietly. The pair moved round the room, depositing explosives at each of the chamber's support pillars. As the final charges were placed, Carson and Wills returned with a stretcher and Kramer was strapped into its canvas.

The four men pulled gas masks from their packs and over their heads, Jones fitting another over the face of the unconscious German. Each man lifted a handle of the stretcher and they slipped out of the bunker and away into the trench complex. They encountered only scattered guards as they negotiated their way through the muddy warren. It seemed Kramer really had thrown the bulk of his men into the assault on Ypres. The remaining Germans eyed the party through the goggles of their masks with little interest – just one more wounded man on his way to the charnel house of the medical tents.

Reaching the point where they had slipped into the trenches earlier, the British soldiers waited. After what seemed an eternity, the flat reports of the demolition charges echoed behind them, the noise accompanied by a faint tremor rippling through the ground. A moment later the klaxons began to sound, mixed with shouts of alarm as the Germans discovered the damage inflicted on their command post. Banking on the distraction providing cover for the final stretch of their escape, Jones and his men hauled their unconscious captive up and over the side. Hoisting the stretcher between them, they stumbled over the uneven ground of No Man's Land towards the distant sound of battle.

As soon as they were out of sight of the trenches, Jones pulled the gas mask from his head and cast it aside, grateful to be free of the heavy canvas hood. His men did the same.

"Not far to the tunnel now chaps," he said.

Being dressed in the uniform of the enemy complicated their return to Imperial lines. Little point in making it all the way back after this foolhardy exercise, only to be shot by their own sentries. The tunnel had been a key element in the plan.

Imperial sappers had gone to work with their drilling machines – rotating rings of iron teeth gouging at the earth, the soil liquefied by hot steam and piped out to the surface. The resulting passage stretched for a mile, stopping short of the deeply-sown mines both sides had peppered across the centre of No Man's Land to prevent subterranean assault. The tunnel's low ceiling had looked set to collapse at any moment and the seeping groundwater made it like crawling through a sewer, but now, nerves jangling, twitching at every crack of gunfire, Jones longed to reach the welcoming safety of the underground passage.

The noise of the guns and explosions marking the German assault grew steadily as the party stumbled onwards. As they scrambled up the last ridge before the tunnel entrance, the sounds of battle were complemented by the drone of engines from the skies above.

The bulk of an airship emerged from the low cloud, the props mounted along the gondola's side tearing swirling holes in the vapour. Engines rumbling, the airship slid down out of the greyness until it loomed massively above them, the dark tan of its gasbag making for an ominous contrast with the red, white and blue markings on the tail fins. The men stared up as the long doors on the underside of the gondola cracked open.

"Get down!" shouted Jones.

They dived for cover, scattering as the bombs fell.

*

Jones stormed into Brigadier Gourlay's office and tossed the hand onto his superior's desk. The appendage was whole enough, if a little dirty, but the wrist ended in a ragged stump with an inch of white bone protruding from the torn flesh.

His commanding officer frowned, leaning forward to give the offending article a poke with the tip of his pen. He looked up at Jones, an eyebrow raised.

"There is a limit to my indulgence you know..."

"The only piece left of Colonel Kramer," said Jones. "Thanks to those blithering idiots in the Aeronautic Corps."

Gourlay cursed under his breath and leaned back in his chair, rubbing at his temples. "You actually had him? Buckingham's crackpot scheme worked?"

Jones pulled out a cigarette and struck a match, willing his hands to stop shaking long enough for him to get his smoke alight. He slumped into the canvas chair before Gourlay's desk and blew a stream of smoke towards the ceiling.

"All credit to the old man," he said around the side of his cigarette, "the plan worked a charm."

"Your friend Kramer might disagree," said Gourlay, nodding towards the grisly remnant on his blotting pad. "What happened?"

"Two minutes from the damned tunnel and one of our own airships dropped a tonne of explosives on top of us. Blew the Colonel into bits, and sent Mackenzie flying. Broke his bloody leg. The rest of us had to carry him."

"Lucky you weren't all killed."

"Don't feel very lucky. All that effort, and for what? Some files and a chunk out of a wireless."

"You're determined to be miserable, aren't you?" said Gourlay. "The Bletchley lot will be delighted to get their grubby paws on that souvenir of yours. They've been in the dark for months since the codes changed. Now they'll be able to read Fritz's love letters again."

"Not quite the same as having a genuine Kraut Colonel to question though, is it?" Jones gave a bitter smile. "I'd love to see the Duke's face when someone tells him what happened."

"You can tell him yourself. He's next door."

"Buckingham? He's here?"

"Arrived just after you left last night. Wanted to see you as soon as you returned." He waved towards the door. "Off you trot. Best run along and see what the old man wants."

Jones pulled himself up. He left the Brigadier prodding at the severed hand and made his way to the next office along the corridor, knocking once before pushing open the door.

The Duke of Buckingham turned away from a bundle of papers. His penetrating gaze gave Jones' dishevelled appearance the once-over. Appraising the goods, thought Jones sourly. Checking I'm still in one piece, checking I'm still useful.

"Glad you're back. Got a job for you." The Duke spoke in his usual brisk style – short, sharp phrases delivered through his moustache like machine gun bullets flying from an ambush position.

"Don't you want to hear about the last one?"

"Already heard. Bloody annoying, but can't be helped."

"Can't be helped? God Almighty," Jones wiped his hand down his face. "You don't seem too bothered one of our own airships wasted more than a month's planning. And almost killed me and my men into the bargain."

The Duke regarded him from beneath a low frown. "And if I indulged my irritation, would it alter the outcome?" He shook his head. "Besides, you obtained the cipher machine."

"But lost the Colonel..."

Buckingham waved the comment aside. "We have another problem. In the Caribbean."

Jones snorted. "We have enough problems right here in France."

"We do indeed. But they'll only get worse if this affair isn't sorted. Dreadful business." The old man got to his feet and shuffled round the table, leaning heavily on his cane. He pointed at the cigarette in Jones' hand. "Give me one of those, would you?"

Jones pulled the metal case from his pocket, popped it open and let the old man extract a cigarette. Buckingham took the proffered matchbox and lit up, sucking in a lungful of blue smoke. Jones dragged a chair over and dropped into it, suddenly exhausted, the tension of the last twenty-four hours catching up with him in a rush of weariness and nerves. Resignation washed over him, coupled with more than a little trepidation – here we go again.

"What's going on? And what has it got to do with me?"

Buckingham stared at him for a long moment before speaking. Jones could tell something must be seriously amiss. Normally the old man relished this moment, the grand unveiling of his latest scheme, but the usual glint in his eye was absent. Jones had never seen the Duke's expression so grave.

"I'm sorry David," said Buckingham. "I have some bad news..."

*

Havana

"Welcome to the Protectorate of Cuba."

The customs official refolded the travel documents and handed them over the desk. Jones nodded his thanks and tucked the passport and visa back into the inside pocket of his jacket. He stepped past the counter and crossed the marble floor of the aerodrome's first class terminal. Passing through the revolving door, he made his way out into the baking Cuban sunshine. The heat was like a physical obstacle, stopping him in his tracks.

The attendant at the rank of automobiles stepped forward with a tug at the brim of his cap. "Cab *senor*?"

"*Si, gracias*." Jones didn't know much Spanish, but he knew enough to be polite.

The man pulled open the rear door of the first vehicle in line and Jones climbed in, taking a seat beneath the striped canopy. The cab driver turned to look at his passenger.

"No bag?" he asked in accented English.

"The airship company will send my trunk along."

The driver smiled broadly. Jones supposed hauling luggage around in this heat was nobody's idea of fun. The driver's grin widened further when Jones gave him the address. The Cuban turned to his controls, opening valves and pushing the drive levers. With a crunch of gears and a sharp squeal from the boiler, the cab moved off.

As they puttered away from the aerodrome, Jones glanced back to see the bulk of the airship looming over the terminal building and its flanking palm trees. His journey across the Atlantic in the massive dirigible had been most civilised. He was going to miss the food.

He quickly realised he would miss the cool winds of higher altitudes even more. The welcome breeze created by the cab's motion proved all too brief as the vehicle mingled with the heavy flow of traffic towards Havana, slowing to little more than walking pace. The air closed in again, thick and heavy.

The palm-lined road was filled with steam tractors, horse-drawn carts, and cabs like Jones' own. Mechanised bicycles zipped here and there between the vehicles, the only conveyance able to move in anything other than intermittent bursts. Jones' driver seemed determined to compete for every inch of road, and they jerked forward in fits and starts. The other drivers were just as aggressive, engine noises and the braying of horse and donkey almost drowned out in a cacophony of shouted curses and angry blasts on horn and whistle.

Jones reached forward and tapped the driver on the shoulder. "Is it always like this?" he called over the din.

"No *senor*. Much better than before. Ever since the Yankees built the new road."

Jones leaned back and plucked his hat from his head, fanning himself with it. He closed his eyes and tried to ignore the noise as the cab jolted on.

The congestion eased as they reached the outskirts of Havana. Most of the heavier vehicles turned off the main road, making for the industrial quarter, its factories and mills marked by a forest of towering chimneys spewing steam and grimy smoke into the sky. The cab continued on towards the city itself.

The road became a broad boulevard running between a frontage of tall, brightly-painted buildings and the sea wall. Across the bay, a fortress squatted atop the cliffs, whitewashed walls gleaming in the sun beneath the red, white and blue of a limp Stars and Stripes.

The cab stuttered to a halt before an imposing three-storey building set back from the road behind a well-kept hedge. The driver hustled round to get the door but Jones was already out of the automobile, gazing up at the ornate frontage of cream and white stonework. Wrought iron balconies faced the sea from the upper floors and gilded lettering above the doorway proclaimed the establishment to be the Mirador Hotel.

Jones pulled a dollar bill from his wallet and handed it over. The driver's grin appeared once more.

"Enjoy your stay *senor*. Don't let the Mirador tire you out..."

The man jumped back into his cab and the vehicle pushed its way back into the flow of traffic, earning a chorus of angry toots and whistle blasts. Jones stood for a moment taking in Havana's riot of colour – the pinks and yellows and creams of the buildings, the white glare of the sand beyond the road, and the bright blue of the water and the sky above. It made for quite a change from the relentless grey of Ypres. Warmer too, he thought, tipping back his hat and dabbing a handkerchief at beads of sweat. Turning away from the shorefront vista, he climbed the steps of the terrace, heading for what he hoped would be the pleasant shade of the hotel foyer.

The air inside the lobby was indeed wonderfully cool, kept circulating over the checkerboard tiling of the floor by a brace of wooden fans. The soft tick-tick-tick of the fans revolving overhead was the only sound. Jones' ding of the reception desk bell echoed round the space.

A young man in a white shirt and black waistcoat appeared through the door behind the desk. He welcomed Jones with an efficient smile and flipped open the register.

"It seems very quiet," said Jones as he filled in his details.

"Actually, we are fully booked at the moment sir," replied the receptionist with only the merest hint of an accent to his English. "However, most guests enjoy a *siesta* during the heat of the afternoon."

"Now that sounds a fine idea." Despite his restful crossing of the Atlantic, Jones still felt bone-tired. It would take more than a few nights to catch up on the sleep he'd missed over months in the trenches.

"You shall find things much livelier in the evening. Might I suggest you join us later for a drink and dinner?"

*

Jones awoke to the noise of other guests stirring and the murmur of conversation floating up past his window from the hotel's central courtyard. He stepped out onto his balcony and watched the sky darken over the water, moving through rich shades of blue and purple before the first stars winked into existence. He checked his watch and returned to his room. Time to get ready.

After dragging a razor across his traveller's stubble, he took a light suit from his trunk, turning it this way and that to check the linen material wasn't too crushed. The bellboy had offered to unpack his things for him earlier, but Jones had waved him away. He had never liked anyone fussing around him, had never felt the need to employ a "gentleman's gentleman", unlike so many of his friends. It had made him something of an oddity in the circles he had moved in before the war – this stubborn insistence on doing everything for himself. There had been gossip about his finances of course, but he didn't care. He could certainly afford the staff – his father's investments had left him very comfortable on the money front – but the thought of having servants at his beck and call simply didn't sit right.

Dressed, he made for the stairs, entering the lobby as a raucous group of young men piled through the front doors. They threw hats and coats at the cloakroom attendant before making for the salon, clearly looking to continue what must have been an afternoon of drinking. Jones thought one or two of them were already in a state of fairly advanced refreshment.

He followed them through into the bar, concerned he was about to wade into some drunken watering hole. A drink would be fine, but he was in no mood to sit amidst the noisy carousing of others. Thankfully, he spotted the group of rakes being ushered through to some private space, the *maitre d'* obviously keen to ensure the young bucks did not disrupt the rather more civilised atmosphere of the main bar.

The salon was filled with high-backed chairs and ornamental palms. Dark wood trim and burgundy leather offered a handsome contrast to the glitter of the gaslight chandelier reflected from the bottles and mirrors behind the bar. The strains of a string quartet drifted from the phonograph in the corner, a background for the general hum of conviviality permeating the room. Most of the seating was occupied, the clientele a mix of gentlemen in suits, and ladies bedecked in what Jones could only assume were the latest fashions. His knowledge in this area was limited – his time in France hadn't included any Parisian shopping excursions.

He perched himself on a high stool at the bar. "Whisky," he ordered, "with ice."

The barman nodded and prepared the drink, using a hand pick to chip chunks of ice from the block melting slowly on the back bar counter. Jones thanked the man and lifted his glass, relishing the chinking sound of the ice as he swirled the bourbon round. Not real whisky of course but, by God, it would do.

He savoured the sweet smoky burn of the spirit and regarded his reflection in the bar mirror. Gaunt. That was how his dear aunt in Richmond would have described him, no doubt prior to insisting he had a nice hot bowl of soup. But despite his drawn and pale face, here he was, very much alive, enjoying a snifter amongst the dandies of Havana.

A fortnight ago, he had been knee-deep in blood-stained mud, creeping into the heart of the German lines, half-expecting not to see another sunrise. The lads of the Queen's Guards would be green with envy if they could see him now. He hoisted the glass in a silent toast to the boys back in France. Wish you were here gents, or at least not there.

He watched the crowd in the mirror as he sipped at his drink. At some of the tables business deals were clearly being conducted – earnest conversations concluded with hearty handshakes and orders for champagne. But observing the room, Jones realised other, more subtle, business was also underway throughout the salon. Every now and again one of the young ladies – and he noticed now they were all young – would whisper in the ear of her male companion and stand, leading him away by the hand through a door at the rear of the room. The departure was sometimes accompanied by nudges and knowing looks from the man's fellows, but more often than not, went unremarked.

Jones was momentarily shocked, and then amused at his own reaction. If the lads in Ypres would have been jealous before, they'd be doubly-so now. These thoughts were interrupted by a presence at his elbow. He turned and found himself looking into a pair of dark brown eyes.

The woman was striking, her penetrating gaze and sharp cheekbones framed by a tumble of black curls. She was clad in emerald silk, the dress shimmering under the light of the chandelier, the figure beneath it either a natural wonder or a marvel of corsetry.

"You must be *Senor* Jones..." she said, the slight Hispanic accent lending an exotic tinge to his most humdrum of surnames. "Our English gentleman visitor."

Jones pushed himself to his feet, bending his head to brush his lips on the back of the proffered hand. "I am indeed," he said as he straightened, "but I am afraid you have the advantage of me."

The dark eyes flashed. "Best be careful I do not make use of it, eh *senor?*"

Unsure how to respond, Jones made do with a polite smile.

She placed her hand on his arm. "Forgive me. I could not resist. My name is Isabella De La Vega. I am the proprietor of the Mirador."

"Then allow me to offer my compliments. From what I have experienced thus far, your establishment is of the highest quality."

"Thank you *senor*. We do try to make our guests comfortable. I hope you will enjoy your stay." She leaned forward, adopting a conspiratorial tone. "Now tell me, what brings you so far from home?"

"I'm a journalist," said Jones, dropping into the story he had agreed with Buckingham. "The Times wants articles from areas of the world untouched by the war. Something to lighten the cares of our readers." He gestured to indicate their surroundings. "I was lucky enough to bag a jaunt to Cuba and the Antilles."

De La Vega tipped her head to the side and regarded him intently. "Such tired eyes. They do not look like the eyes of a writer."

Jones felt his face flush under her keen appraisal, again finding himself at a loss for a response. He was saved from the awkward moment by a loud interruption.

"Son of a bitch! I should have known..."

A tall, broad-shouldered man strode through the bar towards them, arms thrown wide, the smile across his features a mirror of Jones' own. The pair shook hands warmly before Jones returned his attention to the woman at his side.

"My apologies, my friend and I have not seen one another for nigh-on two years. May I introduce Captain John Kowalski? Captain, this is –"

"Oh we've met," said Kowalski. He offered the woman a bow. "How are you Isabella? You miss me?"

Her eyes narrowed, but the tone stayed light. "Havana is not the same when the sailors of the Free Fleet are not in town."

"Heh. Seems to me the Major here was doing his best to keep you entertained –" Kowalski stopped at Jones' pained expression. "What?"

De La Vega turned to Jones, a twinkle in her eye. She lowered her voice. "Don't worry *Major*, your secret is safe with me." She waved a hand and the barman hurried over. "I shall leave you two gentlemen to get reacquainted. Samuel here will look after you. If there's anything else you require, you only have to ask."

With a swish of her skirts the hotel's owner departed. Both men watched her move off, winding her way between the tables, stopping occasionally to speak with one or other of her guests, a hand on a shoulder here, a tilt of the head and flirtatious laughter there, clearly in her element as she worked the room.

Kowalski clapped Jones on the back. "Hardly in the country and already mixed up with the most formidable woman in Cuba. Quick work Major."

Jones rolled his eyes. "We were just talking. Anyway, I have a bone to pick with you..." He waved a hand. "What sort of place is this to arrange a meeting? It's a damned bordello."

"A damned good one too. And that's the point. Isabella wasn't lying – she really will keep your secret. Places like this have to keep secrets – it's how they survive."

Jones considered this statement. Perhaps the Floridian had a point.

"Besides," continued Kowalski, "if I'd known I was meeting such a miserable old Puritan, I'd have picked someplace else. Like maybe a Temperance House?"

Jones returned Kowalski's broad smile. "Perhaps you'll allow this Puritan to buy you a drink?"

"Major, I thought you'd never ask."

*

As ever, the Mirador's kitchen provided an excellent dinner. Kowalski relished his stays here, even more so when he could bill the not-inconsiderable expense to one of the Fleet's clients. Food and drink always tasted better when someone else was picking up the tab. He finished the last tender morsel of his steak and pushed his plate to the side.

"I should have guessed a cryptic telegram from headquarters would see me running into you again. What does his Lordship want this time?"

"He's a Duke," said Jones, dabbing at the corners of his mouth before folding his napkin and placing it on his sideplate.

"His Dukeship then. All I know is his idea of a good time involves other folks getting shot at."

"Not us. Not this time." Jones paused. "Well, not if everything goes to plan."

"Heh. And how often does that happen?"

Kowalski pulled two long cigars from his inside pocket and clipped the end off one. He offered the other to the Englishman.

"I'll stick to these," said Jones, holding up his cigarette case.

"Havana's finest. Cost a damn fortune. You don't know what you're missing."

Both men lit their respective smokes. After taking a few deep puffs, Kowalski regarded the glowing red tip of his cigar, rolling it to and fro and watching the vapours curl upwards before they were swept round, dissolving in the revolutions of the fan blades overhead.

"So, back to this plan which ain't going to see me get shot at..."

The Englishman looked over his shoulder, surveying the dining room. They had asked for some privacy on moving through from the bar and had been seated in a quiet corner of the opulent dining room. The waiters, bustling around in their black waistcoats and long white aprons, were being kept busy by the other patrons. Seemingly satisfied they couldn't be overheard, Jones leaned forward.

"Have you ever been to Tortuga?"

Kowalski coughed on his cigar smoke. "You're kidding, right?"

"I wish I was. I need to take a look at this infamous den of iniquity. And you're coming with me."

Kowalski realised now why the telegram from the Admiral had contained so few details regarding his new assignment. His superior had known what sort of response he would have received.

"There's some decidedly unsavoury characters on Tortuga. Not one of them I'd like to tangle with."

"Jack Rackham?"

"The worst of the lot. A direct descendant of the original Calico Jack and Anne Bonney. Or so he claims. A nasty piece of work and no mistake."

"You've met him?"

"Seen him once. From a distance. I hear it's the safest way."

"How so?"

"They call themselves a democracy over there – got a constitution and everything. Around five years back, Rackham gets himself elected and then hangs each and every man who'd stood against him. One man, one vote – just so long as Calico Jack is the one man in question." Kowalski grimaced. "Best head back to London, Major. Go tell his Lordship to leave Rackham and his pirates well alone."

"And that's been the policy of the Floridian government, and your neighbours to the north, for far too long."

"They don't attack our shipping. They know better."

"And so you'll look the other way while they plunder the ships of other nations..."

"Damn it Major. It ain't like that and you know it. It'd take half the Free Fleet to clear out that hornets' nest. It just ain't worth it." Kowalski shook his head. Didn't the British have more important things to worry about? "What the hell is the problem? They don't go after anything flying a red duster neither."

Jones stared across the table. "Until five weeks ago." He ground his cigarette into the ashtray. "That's when they took the *Milford*, a merchantman out of Bristol. Stole her cargo and used her for target practice. One man survived just long enough to tell the Consul what happened."

Kowalski frowned. He'd heard nothing of this.

"Since then another three British ships have gone missing in the area. No mayday messages. No reports of bad weather. The Admiralty is convinced Rackham and his band of cut-throats are responsible."

"Four ships in five weeks? If it is Rackham, he's not messing around."

"Quite. And why those ships? That's the question. Other British vessels have passed unmolested."

"Any connection between them?"

"Not really. All out of different ports – India, Hong Kong, Jamaica." Jones' brow furrowed. "The only common denominator? All four were carrying arms destined for France."

The two men fell silent as the waiter arrived to clear their dishes from the table. They waved away the dessert menus and Jones waited until their server was well out of earshot before he spoke again.

he Royal Navy tied up keeping u-boats out of ...ntic, we can't spare the ships to come over here and teach Rackham a lesson." He shrugged. "Not that we would of course. The Americans wouldn't appreciate a squadron of dreadnoughts throwing its weight around on this side of the pond. Caribbean is *their* ocean apparently. If we ever hope to get them into the war on our side, we can't afford to upset them."

"But if your navy ain't coming, why are you here?"

"Reconnaissance. I'm here to take a look at Tortuga with you. Between us we have to work out how much it would cost."

A cold knot formed in Kowalski's stomach. "To do what?"

"Her Majesty's government will be securing the services of the Free Fleet, and any of the smaller Floridian mercenary corps which may be required in support. We're going to wipe out Tortuga's little infestation."

"Ain't going to be cheap Major. If it can be done at all."

"We cannot allow any interference with ships coming through Panama. Nor can we allow Rackham's antics to encourage any other miscreants by going unpunished." Jones frowned, a distant look on his face. "It's bloody awful in France at the moment. With Lenin and his chums sitting firmly on the fence, the Kaiser's free to fling everything at us. You won't read it in the newspapers of course, but if we start losing supply ships, it could tip the balance."

"That bad, huh?"

Jones' battle-weary eyes gave Kowalski his answer.

"So why did Buckingham send you? No offence Major, but this sounds like a job for a sailor, not a foot-slogger."

"Two reasons. Firstly, it seems I have a personal relationship with a highly-regarded officer of the Free Fleet." He raised his glass. "That's you by the way. In case you didn't recognise the description."

Kowalski returned the toast. "I'm flattered."

"You should be. I didn't recognise it either."

"Heh. And the other reason?"

Jones' smile faltered. He tipped his head back, draining his whisky. He stared into the empty glass for a long moment before lifting his face to meet Kowalski's gaze.

"Buckingham knew I would insist on coming. The captain of the *Milford* was my brother."

*

The next morning they met for a walk along the Malecon, the wide promenade which divided Havana from the azure waters of the bay. Although the sun was shining, it had not yet heated the air to unbearable levels and a pleasant breeze rolled in over the beach. Well-dressed men and parasol-toting ladies strolled up and down, taking the morning air. Kowalski missed no opportunity to tip his hat to the prettier of the women, earning him a few flirtatious giggles from behind gloved hands, and no end of scandalised tutting from matronly chaperones.

"How's Maria?" asked Jones.

Kowalski's face took on a sheepish cast. "She's good. Up in Boston. Working at the Technological Institute. She's busy. We write one another."

"Please give her my regards in your next letter. Lovely young woman. She'll make some lucky man in Massachusetts very happy I'm sure."

Kowalski scowled and stomped off ahead. Jones smiled to himself before lengthening his stride to catch up. As they approached the harbour, he spotted a dark shape, barely visible in the water offshore.

"What's the wreck?" he asked.

"The *USS Maine*. Can't see much just now, but at low tide her funnels and upper deck come clean out of the water."

"Why hasn't she been broken up for scrap?"

A whole dreadnought's worth of steel, just lying there, practically sitting on the beach – the salvage would have been easy. With stalemate in France, every spare piece of metal in England was being harvested for the war effort. Jones' aunt and uncle were still bemoaning the loss of the railings from their garden wall.

"Don't let any Yankees hear that kind of talk," said Kowalski. "It's a shrine for them. Near three hundred sailors died when the Reds blew her up."

"Sentimental claptrap. It won't bring the men back and it's a waste of good steel."

"Ain't how the Americans feel about it, although I reckon most Cubans might agree. They'd happily see the wreck removed. It's a nasty reminder of history round here. If the *Maine* hadn't gone down, the occupation might never have happened. The Americans were mighty unimpressed at her sinking – she was the pride of their fleet at the time." Kowalski stared out at the wreck and gave a wry smile. "Only ten years ago, and the whole design is near obsolete. Her sister ships are lined up in the breaker yards over at Guantanamo. Seems it's fine for the Cubans to demolish dreadnoughts as long as the Americans are paying for it."

They walked on, the brightly-painted hotels and grand houses giving way to the duller stonework and plain wood of shipping offices, carpenters' workshops and chandlers' stores. Steamships and barges lay moored at every quay, tall freight elevators carrying pallets of cargo up and down between the seagoing vessels and their airship counterparts anchored above. Barrels of oil from the Gulf Coast, sugar from the plantations of Jamaica, coal and ore from the mines of central and southern America – every day the produce of half the world passed through Havana's bustling harbour and airyards.

The two men turned away from the seafront and Jones followed his guide down a cobbled alley, the buildings on either side leaning towards one another overhead, balconies almost touching. The narrow thoroughfares away from the front were packed with people and the pair rubbed shoulders with merchants, sailors and stevedores as they squeezed through the crowds. Gangs of street urchins ran barefoot through the throng prompting a warning from Kowalski to keep a weather-eye open for pickpockets.

After a few hundred yards, Kowalski stopped and pulled Jones into a doorway, a temporary refuge from the press of people. He indicated a tired-looking tavern on the other side of the street, its sagging timbers broken up by grimy windows, impenetrable to the eye.

"Delightful," said Jones. "You're sure this is the best place?"

Kowalski nodded. "I know it don't look like much. In truth, it ain't. But this is where the smuggler captains do their drinking. We need a boat, and a man at the helm who knows the waters and can keep his mouth shut. This is where we'll find him."

*

The walls of the bar were stained a dirty brown. A thick haze of smoke hung in the air, as much a permanent fixture of the place as the leather-faced men whose cigars produced it.

Conversation at the tables around the bar's perimeter died away as the two men entered. Kowalski felt the cold appraisal of the assembly pass over him before the patrons returned to their drinks and muted discussions. Checked over, and dismissed as no immediate threat, the pair made their way towards the counter at the rear of the room. The man slouching at the end of the servery abandoned his newspaper and shuffled over.

"What can I get you gen'men?" The accent was a thick Southern drawl. Mississippi, thought Kowalski.

"Whisky," he said, counting ten dollar bills onto the bar top. "And information."

The grizzled bartender eyed the money, his tongue slipping out to run over cracked lips. "Well now, the drink is no problem." He reached down and pulled a pair of chipped glasses and a bottle from beneath the counter, pouring out two large measures. "The other part? Kind of depends, don't it."

"I just need a recommendation is all," said Kowalski. "My friend and I are looking to take a fishing trip. But someplace more interesting than the usual spots. You know a boat that might be available?"

"Maybe's I do," said the man, scratching at his unshaven chin. "This trip of yours... I guess it might be going off the beaten track. Looking for a secluded cove or somesuch?"

"Something like that." Kowalski placed another five dollars onto the pile.

The barman swept up the money, folding it and tucking it into his shirt pocket. He padded out from behind the bar and over to the tables, bending down to whisper in the ear of one of his customers. He returned with the man in tow.

"This here is Luis. He might be able to help you folks out."

The bartender went back to the counter and his newspaper, leaving Kowalski and Jones regarding Luis. The sailor was short and scrawny, the sleeves of his filthy shirt rolled up to reveal forearms covered in tattoos. Dark hair and a week's stubble framed a weatherbeaten face. The Cuban smiled, revealing a row of gold-capped teeth.

"*Senors*, you are looking for a boat?"

"You have one?" asked Kowalski.

"A most excellent one." Luis looked down at the glasses on the bar. "Let us discuss the qualities of my vessel over a drink."

He waved over the barman and ordered rum. The drink arrived and the sailor crossed his arms, staring at Kowalski, who duly tossed a coin onto the bar top. Luis flashed a golden smile and lifted his glass, leading the way to an empty table situated away from the other customers. They sat, and Luis raised his drink in a salute. Kowalski and Jones both took sips, whilst the Cuban drained the amber liquid in one and smacked the glass back down on the table.

He wiped his mouth with the back of his hand. "You plan a fishing trip, eh? One you would like to be kept private thinks Luis."

Kowalski leaned forward. "Very private. My friend and I are keen to avoid any undue attention."

Luis grinned at them both, metalwork gleaming. "And this is why you need Luis. Nobody knows these waters as well as he." The eyes narrowed. "But Luis has drink to buy and women to rent. These things are not cheap. And neither is Luis..."

Kowalski pulled a wad of money from his pocket and peeled off fifty dollars. He placed it on the table before the Cuban.

Luis looked from the pile of bills to Kowalski. "The cargo you are moving. It is valuable?"

"Valuable to us. It's just me and my friend here."

The sailor jerked his thumb in Jones' direction. "This friend of yours does not have much to say."

Jones stayed silent, sticking to the plan of letting Kowalski do the talking. American accents were commonplace, they didn't need the extra attention his English tones would generate.

"He's a newspaperman," said Kowalski. "Writes more than he talks. He's planning a story about our destination."

A sly glint appeared in the Cuban's eyes. "*Si, si.* Your destination. Luis thinks you would not have left this detail until last if it was not the most important part of the arrangement. The most expensive part perhaps..."

"You already have fifty dollars."

"Enough for Luis to take you many places. But not all places, no."

Kowalski paused. Here we go. "Tortuga," he said. "We're heading for Tortuga."

The Cuban blanched, eyes darting round to see if any of the other patrons had overheard. "*Madre de Dios...*" he muttered, wiping his hand through the grimy sweat on his forehead.

Much the same reaction as my own, thought Kowalski. He pulled the wad of money out once more and counted another fifty dollars out.

"There'll be a hundred more when we're safely back in Havana." The sailor stared down at the bills, golden teeth chewing at his lower lip as Kowalski continued. "You'll take us to the northern shore and drop us someplace quiet. You'll wait twenty-four hours and then we'll all sail away again." He patted a hand on the pile of notes. "Come on Luis. I'm sure you know a sweet little beach that would suit us just fine."

Kowalski watched the internal struggle between greed and fear play itself out behind the sailor's eyes. Greed won.

"Another hundred now," snapped Luis. "And another two hundred when we return. Luis will not do this foolish thing for any less."

The Cuban sat back, folding his tattooed arms across his chest. Kowalski shifted his attention to Jones who gave a curt nod. Kowalski shrugged, turned back to the sailor and handed over the extra money.

"Luis, you have got yourself a deal. Just be glad my friend here is so free with his currency."

The gold-toothed grin remained conspicuously absent as the sailor stuffed the bills away.

"Tomorrow morning *senors*," he said. "Sunrise. You meet Luis at the end of the old pier. It takes all day to make the crossing. You go ashore at dusk. That way we avoid the watchers." He scowled at the pair opposite. "But Luis will not wait a night and a day in that place. He sails the following dawn. With or without his passengers."

Kowalski stared over the table. "You don't want to cross me Luis. Worse things can happen than not getting your extra two hundred."

The Cuban recoiled from the look in Kowalski's eyes. "*Si, senor*," he mumbled.

Jones and Kowalski got to their feet. As they made for the door, Luis called after them, his bravado returning, no doubt boosted by the feel of the bank notes in his pocket. "*Hombres*! You don't finish your drinks?"

Kowalski shook his head in reply and pulled the door open. He watched the Cuban pick up each glass, draining them in turn before beckoning the bartender over. Kowalski sighed as he followed Jones out into the street. He hoped Luis wouldn't try to drink a full two hundred dollars worth of liquor before morning.

*

The next stop on their tour of Havana was in an altogether more prosperous district of the city. The two men strolled through the cobbled expanse of a broad square, past the gurgling dolphins of its fountain and into a wide tree-lined boulevard. Art galleries, clothing boutiques and restaurants ran down either side of the street, and rather than sailors and merchants, the pedestrian traffic was made up of society ladies and well-scrubbed houseboys toting their mistresses' acquisitions.

Kowalski led Jones to a small storefront set back from the road beneath a shady colonnade. The shelves in the windows were draped with intricate timepieces, both classic pocket watches and the newer models designed to be worn on the wrist.

The Floridian pushed open the door and a brass bell jangled cheerfully on its spring. A voice called through from the back shop.

"One moment please..."

Jones surveyed the cabinets lining the walls. Behind the glass, dozens of watches and clocks glittered. Many had been designed to reveal the complicated innards of the mechanisms, as if their maker deemed the jewels and precious metals of their casings merely a decorative addition to the beautiful functionality of the gears and levers themselves. Much as he appreciated the fine craftsmanship on display, he was about to ask Kowalski why they were here when a small bespectacled man bustled through the rear door, rubbing his hands with an oil-stained cloth.

"My apologies, *senors*. I was –" He broke off as he recognised Kowalski. "John! It is good to see you."

The Floridian shook the man's hand. "It has been too long." He gestured towards Jones. "This is Major David Jones, from London. Major, allow me to introduce Ramon Cuervo, the finest watchmaker in the world."

The man tutted at Kowalski, wagging a long finger at him before turning to shake hands with Jones.

"The Captain has always been one for the exaggeration. Pay him no heed." A playful gleam appeared in the eyes behind the thick spectacles. "I'll settle for being the best outside of Switzerland."

"Heh. Don't believe a word of it. False modesty. Ramon has been supplying the Free Fleet for as long as we've been in business."

As he waved the compliment aside, Cuervo's eyes alighted on Jones' watch chain. "I recognise those links," he said with a note of excitement. "A Cartwright, if I am not mistaken. May I?"

Jones pulled the timepiece from his pocket, handing it across to the watchmaker. The man ran his thin fingers over the smooth casing and popped the catch, peering down at the face and hands through his half-moon spectacles.

"Ahh," he breathed in appreciation. "The Nautica. The waterproof model. A lovely piece." He frowned. "Although a little scratched."

"It's travelled some," said Jones. "And been through the odd scrape."

Cuervo returned the watch. "Somewhat like yourself, I would imagine. Especially if you are a friend of the Captain here."

"You've got that right," said Kowalski, "and I reckon the Major would appreciate a look at the special merchandise."

Jones offered the watchmaker a polite smile, unsure what the fuss was about. "Your timepieces must be very fine indeed to generate such enthusiasm."

The other men shared a look and Kowalski laughed. "Ramon don't make us anything as mundane as clocks. He has a sideline in an altogether different area. His, ah, hobby."

The watchmaker moved to his front door, locking it and placing a 'Closed' card in the window. He ushered his visitors past the counter and into the cramped workshop at the rear of the store. The wooden shelving was stacked with small boxes filled to overflowing with springs, cogs, scraps of metal and a hundred different lengths of thin brass screws.

Cuervo reached up to one of the boxes, pulled it aside and fumbled with something at the rear of the shelf. With a click, an entire section of shelving swung back, revealing a steep set of wooden steps heading downwards.

The trio descended the staircase. At the base of the steps, Cuervo flicked a wall switch, bathing the secret cellar in bright light from an electric lamp affixed to the centre of the ceiling.

Jones stared at the merchandise on display. Kowalski slapped him on the back. "A regular Aladdin's cave, eh Major? And a little more our style than clocks."

The cases mounted round the walls displayed the most diverse collection of weaponry Jones had ever seen. A quick survey revealed different calibres of pistols, rifles, shotguns and carbines. Other, more unusual items hung alongside the guns – swords, crossbows, throwing knives and harpoons amongst them. Grenades of all shapes and sizes were stacked in neat pyramids, small black spheres the size of cricket balls alongside heavier canister charges.

Jones even spotted a weapon similar in design to the electrical pistol he had used in France – supposedly still top secret, the latest development from Buckingham's workshops at Bletchley.

Bloody hell, thought Jones, we could fight a whole damned war with just the stuff in this room.

Kowalski stood beside the watchmaker, a broad grin plastered over his face. "Ramon, I want you to fix up the Major with whatever he takes a shine to. My treat."

Jones snorted. His treat indeed. As if any bills wouldn't eventually find their way to London in the extortionate fees the Admiralty would end up paying to hire the Fleet. But he moved over to the cabinets all the same, drawn in by the intriguing arsenal on display.

One device in particular had already caught his eye and he wanted to examine it further. After all, it couldn't hurt to have a little look...

*

"Well Major, here's to a successful fishing expedition."

Jones clinked his glass against Kowalski's and they both took a drink. The salon was still quiet at this stage of the evening, the pair having enjoyed an early dinner with a view to getting a good night's sleep before their dawn departure.

"How's the new toy?" asked Kowalski.

Jones couldn't help but grin as he patted the mechanism running down his right forearm beneath the sleeve of his jacket.

"I must admit I've been amusing myself with it all afternoon. Most fun I've had in months. How did you get on with the rest of the gear?"

"Packed and ready. I doubt we'll need half of it, but it don't hurt to be prepared."

Jones raised his glass again. "Amen to that."

Kowalski's gaze slipped beyond Jones' shoulder. "Look out Major, I think you've been targeted..."

Jones turned to see Isabella De La Vega approaching, her eyes fixed on him, a smile playing at the corners of her mouth. Her hair fell over bare shoulders, the ruby dangling at the end of her necklace contriving to draw the eye downward to the ample charms revealed by the low neckline of her black dress.

Caught up in appreciation of the sight as she progressed across the room it took some time before Jones noticed the uniformed man who followed at her shoulder. He was perhaps fifty, bushy white sideburns on either side of a broad face, the stiff collar of his shirt pushing up into the weighty folds of his chin.

"Good evening *Senor* Jones," said De La Vega. She nodded coolly at Kowalski. "Captain."

"Heh. Charming as ever Isabella," said the Floridian.

The woman ignored him, speaking once again to Jones. "Allow me to introduce Commodore Silas Culpepper of the United States Navy, head of the military here in the Cuban Protectorate." She smiled as the men shook hands. "The gallant Commodore protects us from the perils of Communism."

The American frowned. "Which is no matter for levity, madam." He returned his attention to Jones. "So you're the newspaperman?"

Jones glanced at De La Vega. Her eyes sparkled with mischief.

"David Jones, of the Times. Delighted to make your acquaintance."

"And what drags a reporter away from the war? One would assume Europe has more than its share of stories still to be told."

"Indeed. But sometimes people like to hear something other than war stories."

"My girls would certainly agree with you there *senor*," put in Isabella. "Such tales become quite tiresome after a while. Sailors in particular will talk of little else. As if they have a, how do you say it? A one-track mind."

Culpepper's fleshy face coloured and Jones had to smother a smile. "Perhaps you will allow me to visit your headquarters Commodore?" he asked.

"To what purpose?"

"An interview? I feel certain our readers would be interested in how the American administration runs its occupation of the island."

Culpepper's eyes narrowed at Jones' phrasing. "There is no occupation Mister Jones. Cuba is under my country's protection. I can assure you, aside from all but a small handful of malcontents, the Cubans are very happy my troops and ships are here."

"A handful? I had heard the rebel movement was on the increase."

"And there we have a perfect illustration of the dangers of an unfettered press – a baseless exaggeration of the facts. Our presence here is no different from you British being in Gibraltar or Hong Kong. Take care your opinions are not coloured by the questionable company you keep." He gave Kowalski a sideways look. "These secessionists are always keen to paint the United States in a bad light."

Silent before now, Kowalski spoke up. "It's a pleasure to meet you too Commodore. Your reputation precedes you."

Neither Culpepper nor Kowalski made any attempt to instigate a handshake.

"As does yours Captain. I noted your arrival in Havana with interest. I like to keep appraised of the movements of you mercenary types."

"By my reckoning, you wouldn't even be in Cuba if us mercenary types hadn't been around to sort things out for you a few years back..."

Culpepper scowled. "A course of action I opposed vigorously at the time."

"Ah. Still rankles then, that you needed us folks to help you out?" Kowalski's grin seemed calculated to infuriate the other man.

With a visible effort, the American pulled his temper into check, but the voice remained hard. "Tell me Captain, how long do intend to stay in Cuba?"

Kowalski jerked a thumb towards Jones. "You'd have to ask my employer. After all, I'm just the hired help."

Culpepper glowered at the Floridian before turning to Jones once more.

"You will excuse me. I have another engagement. Contact my office. They will arrange a suitable time for your visit and our interview. In the meantime, try not to let your acquaintance lead you too far astray."

The American bowed to Isabella and strode from the salon.

"So that's the infamous Commodore Culpepper..." said Kowalski.

De La Vega placed her hand on Jones' arm. "My apologies *senor*. When he heard we had a reporter staying, he insisted on an introduction."

"And when a gentleman like that insists," said Jones, "I imagine it's difficult to refuse."

A spark of anger flickered in her eyes. "The *senor* is no gentleman. Unfortunately it is impossible to refuse any of his demands, be they for introductions, money or, ah, entertainment."

"He takes bribes?"

Isabella smiled at Jones' surprise. "This is Cuba *senor*. Everyone takes bribes. The mark of a gentleman is how he asks for the money."

"Heh. In London, I believe they judge a gentleman by how he treats a lady. Ain't that right Major?"

Jones glared at Kowalski who shrugged back, attempting to look innocent. Isabella seemed to appreciate the Floridian's input for once, likely because it opened up a new move in her game. She fixed her gaze on Jones.

"Really? And how would you treat me *senor*?"

Jones searched for an appropriate rejoinder but struggled once again. What was it about this damned woman that made it so difficult for him to talk? De La Vega smiled at his discomfort.

With an exaggerated yawn Kowalski stretched out his arms. "I'm going to hit the sack," he said. "Don't let this one keep you up too late Major." He bowed in the face of Isabella's withering glare and tipped Jones a wink. "Good night folks. I'll leave you to it."

He ambled away, leaving Jones and Isabella standing at the bar.

"You don't like him very much, do you?" said Jones.

She turned to face him. "Neither would you *senor*. Not if his Free Fleet had murdered your brother."

Jones felt the dull ache of his own grief pull at him. "Your brother?"

"A fighter in the Revolution. At least he wanted to be. He was only a boy." She gestured towards the door through which Kowalski had departed. "And they came here and killed him. For money."

"At the behest of the Americans..." said Jones, feeling obliged to defend his friend.

"You are a loyal man, *Senor* Jones. More loyal than he deserves."

"I owe him more than loyalty. He's saved my life. More than once."

"These newspapers of yours must be a dangerous business," she said, forcing a smile onto her face. "You will have to explain that to me at some point." She leaned forward, lowering her voice. "Along with the truth of why you are really in Cuba... Major."

"I fear if I failed to cultivate my air of mystery, I would not receive quite as much of your attention."

The smile this time was genuine. "Come with me," she said, taking his arm and steering him towards the glass doors of the balcony. "We shall look out at Havana and you will tell me of London, and the way English gentlemen treat their ladies..."

*

The twinkling gas lamps of Havana's waterfront curved away on either side of the hotel, the water beyond the sea wall reflecting the silver glow of the quarter moon. Jones found himself neglecting the view in favour of the woman at his side. She stood, hands on the railing, eyes closed, face tilted upwards, breathing in the night air. The dark eyes flicked open and she caught him staring. He dropped his gaze and she gave a throaty laugh.

"Do I scare you that much *senor*?"

Bloody woman. She made him feel like a nervous schoolboy. Jones fumbled in his pocket for his cigarettes, pulling one from the case and striking a match. He turned to shield the flame from the breeze, cupping it in his hands.

When the rough Irish voice sounded behind him, his mouth went dry and the cigarette fell from his lips.

"Turn around slowly, matey. Or I'll slit the whore's throat."

Jones did as instructed, to see Isabella held by the hair, her head wrenched back, squirming as she strained to avoid the blade at her neck. Her assailant gave a growl of warning as Jones stepped forward.

"I'll gut her, I swear."

Jones moved back to the railing and the man shuffled into the light spilling from the salon, pushing Isabella before him. Jones' breath caught in his throat at the man's appearance.

The skin of his hollow, sunken face and hairless head was so pale it seemed almost translucent, the ghoulish whiteness exaggerated in contrast with the rust-streaked metal plate covering half his skull. The man's right eye was wide – bloodshot and lidless within a circular socket formed of riveted iron. Beneath the hideous eye, the mouth opened out into a gaping hole, the cheek almost entirely missing, exposing teeth and gums in a cadaverous grin. Tendons and scarred skin stretched and shifted as the man spoke.

"You're the newspaperman? I've got a message for you."

Isabella twisted in the man's grasp, eyes wide.

"You need to let her go. Right now," said Jones, steel in his voice.

"Or what? You'll write a nasty story about me?"

Jones brought his right arm up. With a flick of his wrist the spring-loaded mechanism strapped to his forearm activated, flinging the derringer pistol from his sleeve and into the palm of his hand. He stared down the barrel of the snub-nosed weapon.

"No. I'll shoot off what's left of your face."

The lop-sided smile faded. "Nice wee toy you've got there matey." The Irishman pressed the knife against his captive's skin and Isabella strained, pulling away from the metal's touch. "Don't make me kill her. Would be a criminal waste of a fine doxy."

Jones' fingers flexed on the grip of the pistol in frustration. He wasn't sure he could take the shot without the man's reflex reaction cutting Isabella's throat.

"Let her go. Then we can put the weapons down and talk like gentlemen."

"Who says I'm a gentleman?"

"We can talk. Or you can die. Last chance."

The man stood, grotesque head tilted to the side, considering.

"All right," he said. "But understand this, you touch me and Jack Rackham hunts you down like a dog. Not to mention what he'll do to your lady friend here. Clear?"

"Understood."

The man withdrew the knife and shoved Isabella forwards. Jones caught her in his arms and looked down, ready to offer comfort. Instead, he found himself restraining the woman as she turned on her attacker, blazing with fury. Spanish curses filled the air as she hurled abuse at the Irishman. The man's left eye narrowed, a frown forming on the mobile half of his face as the stream of insult continued.

"Isabella," snapped Jones, sensing the limit of the man's patience, "Enough."

The interruption seemed to bring the woman back to herself. The rage in her eyes remained, but the voice was cold and level when she spoke once more. "You and your kind are supposed to stay out of my place. Rackham gave me his word."

"I'm not inside now, am I missy? Besides, I'm here on business, not looking for any of your amusements." He waved her aside. "Run along now. The reporter and I need to have words. Like gentlemen."

Isabella spat a final curse and stormed from the balcony, slamming the door behind her hard enough to crack one of the glass panes.

"Fiesty one you've got there. Needs to watch her mouth." The Irishman nodded after her. "Pretty though."

Jones was in no mood for banter. "Deliver your message and get the hell out of here before I change my mind."

"I get so much as a scratch, and Rackham torches this place and everyone in it."

"Ah yes, Jack Rackham – the infamous King of the Pirates."

"There are some as call him that. Others call him Calico Jack. Me? I call him sir."

"And what do they call you?"

"Name's Rook. Ask your friend from Florida about me." He grinned, ghastly, skull-like. "There are stories."

"I'm sure there are. What does Mister Rackham want with me?"

"What do you want with him? More's the question." He continued over Jones' attempt to speak. "Don't deny it now. You hired a boat to take you to Tortuga. Only you hired it from the wrong man."

So much for the fishing expedition. Jones shrugged, trying to hide his frustration. "I write stories. To sell papers. Pirate stories will sell. I wanted to see Tortuga."

"Exactly what I thought. A man getting too nosy is all, I says. Let me have a chat with him, I says." The mismatched eyes stared at Jones. "Encourage the nosy gentleman to be leaving Havana and heading on home before someone gets hurt."

"Message delivered."

"Delivered maybe." Rook raised his knife and tapped the point against his metal plating. "But is it understood?"

Jones' fists itched, but he mastered his anger. "Perfectly," he said through gritted teeth.

The hideous smile reappeared. "Good stuff matey. Because after noon tomorrow, if I sees you in Havana, or Cuba, or anywhere else in the Antilles, I'll kill you. Little toy guns or no." He paused, waiting until Jones gave a reluctant nod. "Now then, I've got to be off. Old Rooky has work to do. Nasty work. Nothing a fine gentleman like you would want to be involved in."

Speech over, he placed his hands on the railing and vaulted off the balcony. Astonished, Jones saw the man land like a cat twenty feet below, spring straight to his feet and walk off with a jaunty stride, sauntering down the Malecon through the patches of gaslight.

Jones watched the Irishman disappear into the night then pushed open the door to the salon. The room was deserted except for Kowalski, crouched down behind the velvet drapes framing the balcony windows.

"Been there long?" asked Jones.

"Long enough." The Floridian stood and tucked away his pistol. "Came downstairs when Isabella started her screeching. It sounded like you had things under control. Didn't want to interrupt."

"So you heard?"

"Most of it. Looks like our boat trip is scuppered. And it don't sound like a healthy idea for you to stay in Havana."

"I'll be damned if I let some messenger boy run me out of town."

"Rook's a bit more than the mail boy. He's Rackham's pet assassin, and he's good at his job. Enjoys it too."

"I have no idea where he appeared from. And the way he jumped off the balcony like some kind of bloody monkey? Not natural."

"Natural definitely ain't the word. Ways I heard it, he was born looking like that and got sold to the circus. Grew up a sideshow freak before graduating to acrobat.

Fell in with Rackham's crew and developed a taste for killing. It was Jack paid to get his face all fixed up."

"Charitable of him..."

"It was worth it. Bought his loyalty. Rook does exactly what Rackham tells him to."

"Well he certainly seems to have my card marked."

Kowalski grimaced. "That he does. But at least we have until tomorrow to get you out of town."

*

Jones sat at the desk in his room, sipping at the tea he had ordered and flicking through the pages of the previous day's Miami newspaper. Isabella had them shipped across the straits for the benefit of the Mirador's English-speaking guests. It could have been a year out of date for all the attention Jones was paying its contents.

The hotel had returned to business as usual after the earlier disturbance, and the sounds of laughter and music drifted up from the salon below. Jones considered heading outside for a smoke, but the thought of unfastening all the bolts put him off. Rook's sudden appearance and the agile fashion of his exit had made him feel quite uncomfortable. The first thing he had done on returning to his room had been to secure the shutters on the balcony doors.

The small desk clock chimed midnight, reminding him he had planned to be fast asleep by now, resting before an early departure. Frustration filled him, mixing with the remains of the nervous energy stirred up by his confrontation with the Irishman. Drinking tea and reading bloody newspapers – he could have been doing that back in London. On a good night, he could have been doing it in the damned trenches, although the newspaper might have been considerably more than a day old.

What the hell was he doing here? On some ridiculous quest to track down a bunch of pirates – like something out of a child's storybook. He had raged at his inability to make a difference in the deadlock of France, wanting to do something, anything. And here he was again – hamstrung by events out of his control. He realised now his vague idea of exacting some kind of personal revenge for his brother's death had masked a deeper desire simply to be useful.

Jones pushed the teacup aside and reached for a tumbler. He grabbed one of the crystal bottles without looking to see what it contained and poured himself a large measure. He gulped a mouthful down. Gin – the bitter taste suited his mood perfectly.

Half an hour and half a bottle later, a soft knocking roused him. He thumped the glass down a little harder than he had intended, and moved unsteadily to the door. A flick of the wrist brought the derringer up into his grip, but as he made to turn the key he acknowledged any miscreant would be unlikely to knock. Better safe than sorry though.

Isabella stood in the corridor outside his room. She had changed out of the black dress from earlier into one of dark red silk, but once again the shoulders were bare and the neckline provocatively low. Jones made a conscious effort to keep his gaze fixed on her face.

"I asked after you earlier. The staff said you were indisposed."

"I needed a bath and a change of clothes after that animal placed his hands on me." She looked over his shoulder into the room. "May I come in?"

He waved her inside. "It's your hotel. I imagine you can go anywhere you like."

Isabella swept past him in a rustle of skirts and a faint trail of perfume. Jones closed the door and then reset the mechanism beneath his sleeve, concealing the small pistol once again.

"An interesting contraption *senor*. I am grateful you were wearing it earlier."

Jones nodded. "A gift from my Floridian friend. Proved itself useful."

The woman brushed at the front of her dress before looking up. "I want to apologise. For the unpleasantness earlier. And for you being forced to rescue me." She frowned. "It is not a position I am accustomed to. The, how do you say it, damsel in distress?"

"Of that I am certain. But please, the apology should be mine. Rook wouldn't have been anywhere near your establishment if it hadn't been for me."

"Perhaps. How will you get to Tortuga now?"

Jones stared hard at her, eyes narrowed.

She gave a sly smile. "Oh please, *senor*. When I left you outside the salon, I ran straight upstairs to the balcony above. It was too good an opportunity to listen in and perhaps unravel some of that mystery of yours."

Jones crossed to the desk and lifted his glass in a toast. "Well played."

"So now I know what you are up to, but I don't know why. I think perhaps it is time you enlightened me, no? It appears you may be in need of more friends."

"And you're my friend?"

"I could be."

"That depends," said Jones. "I got the impression you were already familiar with our visitor..."

She waved a dismissive hand. "Everyone knows Rook."

"And Rackham? How well do you know him?"

Isabella's eyes flashed in anger. "That *pendejo*," she spat. "I know him. I know him from before he became so grand and mighty. I know him from when he was just another smuggler."

"And you have some arrangement with him?"

"My business involves many arrangements with many men. Expensive arrangements." She shrugged. "Culpepper, he takes his payment so I do not receive visits from the police. The customs men, they take their payments so my whisky does not disappear from the quay. And Rackham? He takes his payment so his filth will not darken the Mirador's door."

She poured herself a drink, taking more care over her choice than Jones had earlier. She turned towards him once more. "Yes, I know Jack Rackham, but I am not one of his creatures. I would help you if I could." The playful spark reappeared in her eyes. "Who knows? If you can get rid of Rackham, it could save me a lot of money..."

Jones thought for a moment. What the hell – she knew most of it already. She might even be able to help.

"It's a long story. Take a seat."

Settled, brandy in hand, she listened attentively as Jones spoke. He surprised himself, explaining more than he intended, going beyond the details of his mission, touching on his frustration at the futility of the war in France and his personal reasons for coming to the Caribbean. Her eyes filled with compassion as Jones talked of his brother, and then narrowed as the story drew to a close with his account of the conversation with Rook.

She stood as he finished speaking, crossing the room to stand before the large gilt-framed mirror. She pulled her long hair away from her shoulder and leaned her head to one side. Her reflected gaze met Jones'.

"Tell me, did he leave me with any bruises?"

Jones lifted his drink, holding her look over the rim of his glass. Placing the tumbler down on the desk, he moved to stand behind her, looking down at the flawless skin of her neck and then back to the mirror. He reached a hand up and ran his fingertip along her shoulder. The drink made him feel clumsy, like he was pawing at her, but Isabella closed her eyes and leaned against him. He bowed his head and pressed his lips to her neck.

"No bruises," he said, lifting his gaze once more.

Isabella returned his reflected stare, pushing her body back against his. Her dark eyes shone and when she spoke her voice was low.

"*Senor* Jones, perhaps you could help me out of this dress?"

He turned her and kissed her, hands sliding around her waist as her own moved up to the buttons of his shirt. Her quick fingers made short work of the fastenings and he thrilled as her fingernails scratched down the skin of his chest. He felt giddy, his body flooded with a heady mix of desire and gin.

She pulled out of the kiss and looked up at him. "And there I was, wondering how I might repay you for saving me earlier..."

Jones broke away, lightheaded, breathless – unwelcome notions of chivalry bubbling up amidst his churning emotions, pushing more immediate passion aside. Repay? He didn't want repayment.

He reached up and held the woman's face between his hands, looking into her eyes for a long moment before he spoke. "Another time Isabella."

She stepped back, confused. "Why?"

"Because you've just been held at knifepoint, and because I'm drunk." She stared at him, clearly unsure how to take the rejection. "Believe me," he went on, "I will regret this decision in the morning. But right now, you'd best be going."

Isabella regarded him in silence before giving a crooked smile and stepping forward to plant a small kiss on his cheek.

"Your friend from Florida was right about you English gentlemen." She moved past him, pausing at the door. "Goodnight *Senor* Jones. Another time."

"I hope so."

"As do I." She pulled the door open and swept out of the room.

Jones slumped into his seat, shaking his head in disbelief at what he had just done. He reached for his drink, determined to tranquilise himself into sleep. Raising the tumbler to his lips, his eyes caught on the newspaper heaped on the desktop, a headline leaping out at him: *Great Ship On Verge Of Cable Completion*.

The gin returned to the desktop untouched as Jones' mind began to churn.

*

The Englishman had already finished his breakfast when Kowalski joined him on the terrace. Kowalski waved the waiter over and ordered his usual Havana breakfast, *tostados* and Cuban-style coffee – strong, sweet and with a pinch of salt. Something Jones might have benefitted from instead of his tea. By the looks of him, he'd not had a lot of sleep.

Order placed, Kowalski regarded the bay beyond the sea wall. The lack of breeze left the water looking like a sheet of glass.

"Would have been a perfect day for that fishing trip," he said.

Jones glanced up at the cloudless blue sky. "It still could be. Just not the one we had planned."

"So you ain't following Rook's advice?"

"Oh, we'll be getting out of Havana. But return to London? Not bloody likely."

They fell silent as Kowalski's breakfast was served. He nodded his thanks to the waiter and sipped at his coffee, waiting until the man moved away before speaking.

"Why do I think I'm not going to like whatever it is you've come up with?"

Jones adopted a hurt expression. "Come now Captain, where's your sense of adventure?"

Kowalski waved in the direction of the sea. "Going that way. With my sense of self-preservation."

Jones pushed the folded newspaper across the tablecloth, tapping his finger on one of the columns. As Kowalski read, the Englishman sipped at his tea.

Kowalski finished with the article. "Yesterday we failed to hire a fishing boat, and now you're looking to commandeer one of the most famous ships afloat? You need to lay off the booze Major."

Jones waved a hand dismissively. "A matter of a telegram or two. The Admiralty will arrange the details. The tricky part will be getting out to her without Rackham's eyes and ears finding out what we're up to."

"We start sniffing around the docks again, you've got to reckon Rook's going to hear about it."

The Englishman nodded. "Exactly so. But I'm hoping the solution to our little problem will shortly be joining us for breakfast." He looked up over Kowalski's shoulder. "And here she comes now..."

Kowalski turned to see Isabella descending the steps from the hotel to the terrace. The two men stood as the woman joined them. She settled into her seat and nodded a good morning to Kowalski, her greeting less frosty than he had expected.

He had never understood the woman's antipathy towards him. As far as he could remember he'd done nothing in the Mirador to invoke her displeasure. Granted, that was no guarantee he was blameless. He'd had his fair share of evenings within her establishment where his recollection was less than complete – it was that kind of place. He smiled back at her over the table, wondering if this represented some sort of thaw in relations. Maybe Jones had put in a good word for him.

"So *senor*," said Isabella, turning her attention to Kowalski's companion, "it was a pleasant surprise to receive your breakfast invitation. Especially as our evening was cut short." She laid her hand on Jones' arm. "We must pick up where we left off sometime."

Kowalski thought his friend seemed uncomfortable. A little hot under the collar there, Major. Jones was a hell of a man in a fight, but when it came to women, or this woman at least, he was like a babe in the woods. Isabella smiled as Jones coloured. Like a she-wolf sizing up her prey.

"But such pleasantries can wait for now," she said. "What can I do for you this fine morning?"

*

They climbed down from the cargo bed of the wagon, Jones reaching up to assist Isabella's descent.

Their escorts marched them down the muddy track serving as the village's main street. The buildings to either side were pocked with bullet holes and blackened with scorch marks. The place had come under heavy attack, and relatively recently, thought Jones, taking in a blood-spattered wall, the stain still fresh enough to attract a swarm of flies.

They saw no one as they made their way to the centre of the village, a small square before the steps of a whitewashed church. The guards motioned them towards the chapel, taking up positions behind the visitors, fingers as ready on the triggers of their carbines as they had been since meeting the wagon on the forest road an hour before.

Jones' suspicion that Isabella maintained contacts with the Cuban rebels had proved correct. Hardly surprising, the woman seemed to know everyone. She had agreed to set up a meeting and arranged for Jones and Kowalski to be spirited out of the Mirador – inside a laundry wagon of all things, hopefully foiling any watchers Rook might have put in place.

Now she smiled warmly up at the extravagantly-moustachioed man in khaki fatigues who emerged from the dark interior of the church.

"General Estrada," she said, stepping up and kissing the soldier on each cheek. "You look well. Life on the run must agree with you."

The man blinked at her use of English, glancing at her companions before answering in the same tongue.

"The food is not as good as it is in Havana. But I survive." He looked her up and down. "Naturally, you look as fine as ever. Providing for the decadence of the Imperialists clearly agrees with you." He shifted his attention. "And these are the Englishmen you insisted I talk with?"

Jones stepped forward, hand outstretched. "Only one Englishman, I'm afraid. David Jones. Pleased to make your acquaintance..."

His voice tailed off as he saw the expression on the General's face change, the dark eyes hardening as they fixed over Jones' shoulder. The Cuban released Jones' hand, hawked noisily, and spat into the dirt. He turned on Isabella, unleashing a stream of Spanish invective, too fast and furious for Jones to catch even a word. Isabella responded in kind and the volume rose to match the passion in the voices.

Kowalski stepped up to Jones' side. "Sorry Major," he said, keeping his voice low as the argument raged back and forth. "Might have been best if you'd left me in Havana. Don't reckon our man is too impressed with Isabella dragging me along."

Jones waited until the verbal combatants paused for breath. "*Senor*," he interrupted, "please listen to my proposal. I promise it will be worth your while."

The man glared at Jones. "You will find we are not so easily bought and sold. You think we too are mercenaries?" He spat on the ground once more. "Come with me. Come and see why I have more pressing concerns than the earning of blood money."

With a venomous glance at Kowalski, the General turned, stomping off towards the church. Isabella watched him go, hands on her hips, exasperation in her eyes.

"Pig-headed fool. He thinks his principles alone will feed his men and provide them with ammunition." She shook her head. "He'll come around eventually, but we may have to endure more of these performances."

"Let's get after him then," said Jones. He turned to Kowalski. "And you, best keep your mouth shut."

The air inside the church was cool in comparison with the baking heat outside. Their eyes adjusted to the dim interior and they became aware of the figures crammed into the pews. It appeared the entire population of the village was huddled inside the chapel.

Jones and Kowalski followed Isabella up the central aisle, taking in the blood-stained bandages and makeshift splints. It seemed as if every one of the assembled men, women and children had suffered some form of injury. At the head of the chapel, before the dais, Jones counted twelve still forms laid out, shrouded in blankets. Half of the lumps beneath the cloth were smaller, child-sized. A kneeling friar in a black robe glanced up as they passed by before turning back to the corpses and his prayer.

They joined the General where he stood before the altar, head bowed. Estrada crossed himself, and turned away from the hanging crucifix.

"I spend my entire life telling the people religion is part of the machinery keeping them prisoner..." He indicated the bodies on the floor. "And yet, in response to this, I find myself praying for their souls."

"What happened here?" asked Jones.

"Men came. In the night. Bandits. They take what little these poor folk have, and kill any who resist." Anger burned in Estrada's eyes. "And the Yankees? They do nothing."

"This has happened before?" asked Jones.

"*Si, si*. Every couple of weeks another village is raided." The General sighed, lowering himself to sit on the topmost step of the dais. "The Americans say Cuba is their Protectorate, and yet the only protection these people receive is what little I can provide. We have spread men around the villages, hoping their presence will keep the raiders at bay." He grunted. "It does not work. Three of my soldiers lie beneath those blankets..."

A small girl in the front pew began screaming, repeating the same phrase over and over. Her mother shushed her, rocking her back and forth, smoothing her hair, comforting her until she fell silent. The girl stared out from the shelter of her mother's arms. Jones dreaded to think what terrible memories she was reliving.

Estrada shook his head. "She's been like that for hours. The same thing each time: *El diablo de hierro...*"

"The iron devil..." translated Isabella.

Jones' mind returned to the scene on the balcony the previous evening: *Old Rooky has work to do.*

"General, perhaps we have more in common than we thought..."

*

Tortuga

Captain Turner stepped out of the wheelhouse to the starboard wing of the bridge. He felt the vibration beneath his feet die away as the great paddles of his ship ceased their labours and the vessel began to slow, carried forward for the moment by her considerable momentum. Turner pulled his pipe from his pocket and stuffed its bowl. Striking a match, he held it to the tobacco and gave out a series of sideways puffs of smoke. He scanned the horizon to the south, grinding his teeth on the pipe's stem in irritation.

"Any sign of our guests sir?" asked Jenson, his First Officer, joining him at the rail.

"Not yet," replied Turner, checking his pocket watch, "but we're early."

"What do you think it's all about?"

"Damned if I know. But it's a bloody nuisance."

"We were well ahead of schedule. A few hours delay shouldn't cause us too much trouble."

Turner was unconvinced. The message thrust into his hand by the wireless operator an hour previously had been short and annoyingly opaque, even by the standards of the dolts staffing the company's offices: a set of co-ordinates, a rendezvous time, and instructions to set his vessel at the disposal of the men he would take on board. It smacked of a longer delay than Jenson's few hours.

The wireless message and the resulting conversation with his distinguished passenger had accomplished what supply problems, two hurricanes, and the outbreak of a war had singularly failed to do. For the first time in two years, the pistons and gears of the equipment running the near seven hundred foot length of his ship were still.

No engineers tended the machinery, no crewmen scurried across the deck beneath the five towering funnels and, worst of all to Turner's thinking, no thick black cable paid out over the stern into the waters of the vessel's wake.

The *SS Great Eastern*, the largest ship the world had ever seen, now sat idly in the Bermuda Strait waiting to take on passengers like some kind of pleasure cruiser.

"Look sir," said Jenson, pointing to starboard.

There, over the bow of their Royal Navy escort, a black speck could be seen against the bright backdrop of the sky. Turner drew out the expanding tube of his telescope for a closer look. Sure enough, one of those whirlybird contraptions. He snapped the eyeglass closed. Well, at least they were on time.

"Make sure that thing stays clear of the funnels and masts," he said. "I don't want it flapping around the deck and breaking something."

"Aye sir," replied Jenson, heading for the stairs.

Turner watched the ornithopter's approach with a frown. He'd flown in plenty of airships in his time, but nothing would encourage him to strap himself into one of those things. He disliked the way the twin rotors above the cab thrashed at the air. It seemed a most aggressive means of achieving flight, a violent beating of gravity into a temporary and grudging submission.

The incoming aircraft swept in low, the downwash from the rotors whipping spray from the surface of the water, the man at the controls leaving it to the last possible moment before pulling up in a steep climb to crest the forty foot wall of the *Great Eastern*'s riveted hull. The ornithopter slowed to a near hover as it passed over the ship's rail, its wheeled undercarriage six feet above the planks of the deck. Waved in by members of the crew, it inched forward and down between the two aftmost smokestacks. The wheels hit the decking and the pilot eased back on the throttle, the rotors' manic spin dropping in tempo.

The door on the ornithopter's flank swung open and three figures hopped down from the aircraft, the leading pair each carrying a pack. The trio crouched low to avoid the spinning tips of the rotor blades and scuttled to where Jenson stood waiting. After exchanging handshakes, the group watched as the ornithopter's engine note rose and the rotors flailed at the air with renewed force.

The aircraft bounced once on its rubber wheels and pulled itself into the sky. The new arrivals waved to the departing pilot and Turner was irked to see his First Officer doing the same. He'd have to have words with Jenson regarding that overly-cheerful demeanour of his. Turner tapped the embers out of his pipe and turned away from the scene below, heading for the bridge, feeling no desire to observe the flying machine's departure.

If the engine room deep within the hull was the fiery heart of the *Great Eastern*, the wheelhouse was its calm, efficient brain. Racks of gleaming brass gauges were patrolled by crewmen, jotting their readings down in leather-bound journals, monitoring the performance of the vessel's automated machinery. Turner ran a tight ship, based on a strict routine, and it was gratifying to see the men continuing their regular procedures despite the distraction of their unusual rendezvous. He passed through the compartment, nodding to the crew and running his own critical eye over the dials.

He paused to speak to the man standing watch by the chart table. "Inform Lord Brunel our visitors have arrived."

"Aye sir," answered the sailor with a crisp salute before turning for the door.

Turner frowned down at the chart and the markings on the glass pane holding it flat. He followed the line of the cable they had already laid, and its transition into dots illustrating the work still to be done. His irritation grew once again. What could be so important for the Admiralty to commandeer his vessel, keeping her and her crew from the task in hand?

He headed for the companionway. He would receive his new passengers in the ship's stateroom. Maybe there he would get some answers.

*

Jones faltered for a moment during the round of introductions, unsure exactly how to describe Isabella. He eventually settled on introducing her as his "associate from Havana." Her eyes twinkled at this, but she resisted any temptation to embarrass him before their new hosts, much to Jones' relief.

The woman had been determined to accompany Kowalski and himself out to the *Great Eastern*. Joining the expedition was her price for putting them in touch with the Cuban rebels and negotiating the deal to borrow an aircraft and pilot. She insisted she was coming along, unwilling to miss out on the twin opportunities of taking her first ornithopter flight and spending time aboard one of the most famous ships afloat.

She also appeared to relish the prospect of taking up a position, however briefly, as a clandestine agent of the British Empire. Now the newest, and perhaps most unlikely, of Her Majesty's special operatives sat on a sofa in the opulent surroundings of the *Great Eastern*'s stateroom, in a striking, if slightly scandalous, outfit of leather boots, riding breeches and a man's cream shirt, unbuttoned at the neck and complemented with a white silk scarf. Something she had "thrown together", as she put it. Apparently an aeronautic excursion required a quite-specific style of clothing.

Far from being the distraction Jones had feared, Isabella was turning out to be something of an asset. He had been worried the officers aboard would be less than impressed with the commandeering of their vessel, but as De La Vega deployed her formidable social skills, it became clear their hosts were enchanted by her presence. The two men were practically falling over themselves to make their female guest comfortable and this warm welcome appeared to extend to her two companions.

As Captain Turner leaned forward to refresh Isabella's coffee, Kowalski caught Jones' eye and gave him a wink. Clearly the Floridian too had underestimated the usefulness of having the woman along. After fussing over the cups and saucers, Turner seemed satisfied

Isabella had everything she required. He turned his gaze on Jones.

"Now Major, perhaps you can tell us what all this is about?"

"Yes, please enlighten us," said Lord Brunel, the old man's frail appearance belied by the strong voice. He adjusted the control stick jutting from the arm of his mechanical wheelchair. The conveyance turned, bringing its occupant around to face Jones, a wisp of steam puffing upwards from the boiler behind the seat, mixing with the trail of smoke from the man's cigar."The message from my offices contained little information."

"My apologies. The Admiralty kept details to a minimum, worried our wireless signal could be intercepted. And further apologies for this interruption to your great endeavour."

Turner harrumphed into his coffee, his frown confirming Jones' suspicions. Isabella notwithstanding, the *Great Eastern*'s captain was clearly unhappy with their presence. Brunel however waved the apology aside.

"The world has made do with telegraph and wireless for long enough. It can wait a little longer for my optical cable. What can we do for you?"

Jones launched into his tale, outlining their need to get a look at Tortuga, and how the task had been complicated by the intervention of Rackham's henchman. Brunel and Turner listened in silence until Jones finished speaking.

"I understand your predicament," said Turner, "but I am unsure as to how we can be of assistance. The loan of our naval escort would seem to run the risk of antagonising the Americans."

"With the greatest respect to the *Iris*," said Jones. "She's getting a little long in the tooth. If she was fit for anything more than light duty, she'd be on the other side of the Atlantic."

Kowalski spoke up. "A single cruiser wouldn't do us any good. Too big to get in unseen, and likely too small to cope with Calico Jack's fleet."

Turner gave another unsatisfied grunt. "So what exactly is it you need? This ship is hardly suited for any kind of clandestine approach."

Brunel plucked the cigar from the corner of his mouth and answered the captain's question before Jones could speak. "It's painfully clear what the Major needs. He's not after the *Great Eastern*." The eyes sparkled. "He wants to borrow the *Neptune*."

Jones smiled back at the man in the wheelchair. Even at eighty years of age it was obvious the precise, inquisitive mind of the great engineer remained as sharp as a tack.

"If you wouldn't mind..."

The old man's face lit up in boyish enthusiasm. "Would you like to see it?"

*

Leaving the plush surroundings of the stateroom, they followed in the wake of Brunel's chair down the companionway to an elevator descending into the depths of the ship. The indicator gauge clicked through the levels, settling on the lowest, and the brass-plated doors slid open onto an enormous space. The *Great Eastern*'s engine room was a vast cathedral to steam power, crisscrossed by piping and walkways, dominated by a series of piston heads connected to the massive crankshafts cutting across the chamber.

The pistons were still for the moment and crewmen clambered around the engines, taking the opportunity afforded by the temporary halt to make adjustments and apply a thick layer of grease to parts normally inaccessible. The atmosphere was filled with the smell of oil, warmed on still-hot metal. The shouts of the engine crew and the banging of tools echoed around the steel cavern, prompting Kowalski to imagine the fearsome din that would fill the space when the engines were running.

Isabella leaned down to speak to Brunel. "This ship of yours *senor*, it is most impressive."

"It's not really mine, my dear. I only designed her. She properly belongs to the blasted accountants who seem to run my affairs. And of course to Captain Turner here, who makes a very fine job of looking after her."

Turner puffed up at the engineer's praise. "His Lordship is too modest as ever. Thanks to his design, the *Great Eastern* practically sails herself. Much of her machinery is controlled by automated mechanisms. Stoking the boilers, trimming the ballast, laying the cable – all mechanical. We can run the whole shebang with a skeleton crew in comparison with other vessels." He gestured along the walkway towards a bulkhead door in the forward wall. "This way please..."

The party traversed the engine room, above the heads of the engineering crew and the gleaming machinery. Turner spun the wheel on the watertight door, swinging it open on oiled hinges. They passed through into a small compartment, square and featureless save for another heavy door, a twin to the entrance. The first door was sealed behind them before the next swung open accompanied by a hiss of air. Turner ushered them through.

This new chamber was of lesser dimensions than the engine room, but was no less impressive. What immediately captured the eye was the pool of water in the floor. Surrounded by a low wall, the circular pool was a full fifty feet in diameter, its cloudy green waters lit from below. It took a moment before Kowalski realised the source of the pool's illumination was the sunlight beating down on the ocean's surface beyond the hull and filtering round beneath the bulk of the vessel.

He stared at the water in consternation before looking up to see equally pensive expressions on the faces of Jones and Isabella. Turner and Brunel shared a chuckle, clearly used to the effect the sight of a gaping hole in the bottom of the ship had on visitors.

"Don't worry," said Brunel. "The excursion pool is quite safe. All a matter of balancing the pressures."

Kowalski's attention was next drawn to the machine hanging above the impossible pool, suspended on thick iron chains with links as long as his arm. Whilst he had some experience with submersibles, he had never seen anything like this before.

The rear of the contraption was a chubby cylinder, perhaps twenty feet in length and fifteen across, a series of round portholes punctuating its riveted plates, and a pair of gleaming brass propellers protruding from below. The forward portion of the craft was a boxy section with six complicated leg mechanisms, three per side protruding out and down, each a mass of cogs and pistons, and ending in a circular plate of thick metal.

A large dome of glass bulged outwards at the front – ten feet wide, crossed over with reinforcing straps of steel. The glass was surrounded by a circle of electric lamps, obviously designed to illuminate the dark depths into which the vehicle would descend. On either side of the bulbous viewport hung mechanical arms, similar in construction to the legs behind, but terminating in heavy pincer claw attachments.

The three visitors gazed up in amazement. Brunel gestured towards the vessel. "There it is. The *Neptune*..."

"I'd read about it, of course," said Jones, "but the reality is much more impressive than the descriptions."

Kowalski leaned towards him. "This is your plan? A steam-powered langoustine?"

Jones shrugged. "I figured if we couldn't sail to Tortuga, perhaps we could walk..."

*

The *Great Eastern* and her escort steamed south as the sun disappeared below the horizon. The two ships anchored over the horizon from Tortuga, beyond sight of any observers on the island's peaks.

Chains rattling, the *Neptune* was lowered closer to the surface of the pool, now turned an inky, dangerous black. A gangplank was laid down and the crewmen filed over, descending into the craft's interior through a hatchway in its metallic carapace. Jones and Kowalski followed, carrying their gear. Jones nodded up to Turner and Isabella who observed from the gantry above. The gesture was returned with a salute from the *Great Eastern*'s captain and stony indifference from the woman.

Isabella had begun with flirting and ended with a stream of Spanish cursing in her campaign to persuade Jones she should accompany them in the submersible. His flat refusal to even consider such an idea apparently confirmed him as the worst kind of chauvinist, revoking his previous privileged status of "English gentleman."

Brunel wheeled up the ramp behind him. "You seem to have disappointed your lady friend Major," he said, noticing the direction of Jones' gaze.

"So be it. This isn't a pleasure cruise. Miss De La Vega needs to learn she can't always get what she wants."

The old man gave a curt laugh. "Not a lesson she will appreciate, unless I am very much mistaken."

Jones looked up once more at the feisty woman from Havana. She glared down at him, arms folded. "No," he sighed, "probably not."

With a deep-throated rumble, the submarine's engines sprang into life, the noise echoing off the walls of the compartment. Jones returned his attention to the man in the wheelchair.

"Thank you for coming to see us off. It wasn't necessary. You and Captain Turner have done more than enough."

"I'm not seeing you off," said Brunel, shifting his control stick and manoeuvring the chair off the ramp and onto the *Neptune*'s plating. He smiled around the stub of his cigar. "I'm your pilot."

With a loud clunk, a square section of the hull began to descend into the submersible, carrying the chair and the engineer with it.

"One of a kind, ain't he?" said Kowalski as he followed Jones towards the hatch.

The *Neptune*'s interior was a cramped collection of passageways dotted everywhere with valve wheels and pressure gauges, a jumble of machinery affixed to every available surface. The low ceilings were lined with a twisted mass of piping, as were the bilge spaces visible through the metal grille of the floor. Jones and Kowalski ducked their heads and made their way forward through the narrow companionway, squeezing past crew members busy making minute adjustments to controls and checking the readings on hundreds of dials.

Only when they reached the control room was there headroom to stand up straight. They entered the chamber at the front of the vessel as Brunel's chair locked itself into place before the curved window. He waved his passengers forwards, the boyish grin once again animating his features as he gestured to the complex array of switches and levers running beneath the viewport.

"This might be the best damned thing I ever built." He patted the small wheel of the *Neptune*'s helm. "I can't resist the slightest opportunity to take it out."

"What is it used for? Other than your own entertainment?" asked Kowalski.

"Surveying the bottom, checking the lie for the cable. We've used its charges to flatten a few seamounts, and we've repaired a couple of breaks too. Make no mistake, this little beastie has proved itself very useful."

Brunel reached up and flicked a switch. The vessel gave a lurch, dropping a foot or so before jerking to a halt. Both his passengers grabbed for handholds, prompting the engineer to give out another bark of laughter.

"Don't worry gentlemen. It's a smooth ride, all the way to the bottom."

"How deep?" asked Jones.

"Three thousand feet here. Should be interesting. We've never been below two and a half before."

"Great," breathed Kowalski.

"Fret not Captain," said Brunel. "The *Neptune* can withstand the pressures of a five thousand foot dive."

"I'm mighty glad to hear it."

"Besides, if it can't cope, we won't know a damn thing about it. The water will crush us like an eggshell in less than a second."

Kowalski gave Jones one of his "What have you got me into?" looks, but Jones ignored him.

Their elderly pilot ran his fingers over the controls, adjusting valves here and there. He opened the cover on the speaking tube mounted above his console.

"All hands, all hands, the clock is set at ten hours."

"What clock?" asked Jones.

Brunel pointed up at a large brass gauge mounted prominently above the other dials. Its face was surrounded by digits, like a regular clock face, although the vertical indicator needle pointed to a ten in the topmost position rather than the usual twelve.

"Our air supply," said Brunel. He pulled a new cigar from his waistcoat pocket. "Thirteen hours if I gave these up of course." He grimaced. "But some prices are simply not worth paying."

The engineer reached up and threw a lever. With a loud clunk, the chains disengaged and the *Neptune* smacked down hard into the surface of the pool. The submersible wallowed for a moment then began to sink, the water travelling swiftly upwards over the glass of the dome.

In seconds the light from the chamber inside the *Great Eastern* was gone, disappearing above them as the *Neptune* began its long silent fall towards the ocean floor.

*

Fifteen minutes had ticked from the air supply clock before a gentle bump announced their arrival on the bottom.

Brunel checked a gauge. "Well, here we are. Let's see what we can see."

He turned a dial on the control panel. The ring of electric lamps around the observation dome burst into life, throwing a harsh white light across the featureless sand. The sudden illumination startled a handful of fish, the silver shapes flitting away into the surrounding darkness.

In truth, Jones was a little disappointed by the view. He wasn't sure quite what he'd been expecting, but probably something a touch more dramatic. Kowalski leaned forward, peering out. He too, appeared nonplussed by the sights. He became a touch more animated when a drop of water fell on his shoulder from a riveted joint in the hull above.

"Your Lordship..." he said, an edge of panic in his tone.

Brunel glanced round to see both his passengers staring in alarm at the damp patch on the Floridian's shirt. "Condensation old chap. Nothing to worry about."

Jones and Kowalski shared a relieved glance and their pilot returned to his controls. Brunel checked the compass, pushed on the drive levers, and spun the *Neptune*'s wheel. The submersible began to stride forward over the sand. The noise of machinery echoed up from the rear compartments, and Jones felt the engine vibration through the soles of his boots, but there was little of the jostling or lurching he had expected from being inside a walker.

"Smooth ride, Your Lordship," said Kowalski, clearly thinking the same.

"Six legs rather than four. That's the secret. Makes us faster too."

"Heh. Faster will suit the Major here. Damned if he ain't always in a hurry."

Brunel turned to Jones. "Five hours or so and we'll be coming up on the north shore of Tortuga. No trenches to slow us down in these parts. We can engage the screws and hop over a trench if we need to, but we're faster if we stay on our feet, and a damned sight more fuel efficient to boot. Besides, the *Neptune*'s an ungainly beast when it's forced to swim."

The conversation trailed off, the three men falling silent as the sinister shape of a shark drifted into view. No doubt attracted by the lights, the grey form kept pace with them as they traversed the seabed. At least a dozen feet in length, it slipped effortlessly through the water alongside the submersible. Twice it flicked across in front of them, jagged teeth jutting from its jaws at random angles, the black beady eye staring in at the men behind the glass.

"Ugly beggar," grunted Brunel. "But seeing things like this is one of the reasons I love the bloody *Neptune* so much."

After sizing up the submersible and apparently establishing it wasn't digestible, the predator turned away. With a flick of its sickle tail, it disappeared into the darkness beyond the reach of the lamps. Jones shuddered as the shark vanished. The brutal efficiency of its shape coupled with the fearsome mouth left no doubt as to its purpose – evolved, if Mister Darwin was to be believed, over hundreds of thousands of years into nature's perfect killer. He hoped to God his brother had drowned before those things had got to him.

"I've seen sharks before," he said. "But never up close. Not sure I cared for the experience."

"You sure don't want them any closer," said Kowalski. "Unless they're on the grill. Nothing beats a shark steak at a cookout."

Both Jones and Brunel stared at the Floridian.

"What?" he demanded.

Brunel voiced the shared sentiment of the two Englishmen. "You colonials really will eat absolutely anything, won't you?"

The hours slipped past as the *Neptune* bore them over the featureless seabed. Only as they approached the coast of Tortuga did the view from the dome change, the level bottom giving way to chunks of rock and tall formations of coral as the ocean floor angled upwards. Brunel slowed the pace of their advance, skirting the larger chunks of rock and taking more care with the *Neptune*'s footing as they left the smooth sand behind.

This was more like it, thought Jones. Or at least, more like the tropical depths of his imagination – filled with brightly-coloured fish weaving between swaying fronds of seaweed, seeking refuge from the nocturnal predators of the reef. The night-time hunters themselves shied away from the lights of the *Neptune* as it strode through their domain – an octopus curling its tentacles into the shelter of the coral, a cruel-looking eel withdrawing into its dark hole. The observers spotted no more sharks, for which Jones gave thanks, mindful of the swim awaiting Kowalski and himself at journey's end.

With the depth gauge reading fifty feet, Brunel flicked off all but one of the lamps, leaving them creeping onwards and upwards preceded by a single patch of light.

"Don't want the Blackpool Illuminations rising from the sea, do we? Not likely to help a clandestine arrival."

"Indeed," replied Jones. He glanced up at the air supply clock above them. Four and a half hours had passed. "We've made good time."

"I promised to deliver you before dawn Major, and if there's one thing I can't abide it's a lack of punctuality. Height of rudeness."

"No complaints from us on that front," said Jones.

"I should hope not. It will still be nice and dark up top. We'll see you safely onto the beach and run the pumps to replenish the air flasks for our return to the ship."

Jones nodded. "And we'll take our little stroll and be back at high tide tomorrow morning."

"It would be just swell if you were here too, Your Lordship," chipped in Kowalski. "Elsewise we're swimming home."

Brunel's smile reflected back from the curved interior of the viewport, illuminated by the red ember of his cigar.

The *Neptune* climbed the slope of the shore until the silvery underside of the surface came into view, lit from above by the thin moon. Ghostly beams shone down from the undulating surface, a shifting dapple of light playing over the sand and rocks around them. Brunel extinguished the last of the lamps and the *Neptune* crept forward until the shimmering boundary between air and sea was only inches above the top of the glass viewport.

The engineer's fingers danced along a row of switches, flicking them down, one after the other. He reached out and turned a valve wheel. With a gentle hiss, the *Neptune* settled, its machinery still for the first time since they had touched bottom following the long drop into the depths beneath the *Great Eastern*.

"Gentlemen, your destination awaits. The upper hatch should be clear of the water."

"Then we shall take our leave," said Jones. He and Kowalski shook the outstretched hand of the old man and headed for the companionway.

"Three o'clock tomorrow morning," called Brunel after them. "Don't be late."

*

The two men swam the thirty feet to the beach, pushing their floating packs before them, then crawled forward out of the gentle surf. Jones lay flat on the sand, the chill night air causing his skin to tingle as the lukewarm seawater ran from his skin. The waves hissed as they lapped against the shoreline, the chirping click of cicadas in the trees the only other sound.

He peered left then right down the beach, discerning no movement. He whispered an all clear to Kowalski and both men rose, crossing the sand in a crouching run, dragging their gear into the cover of the palms edging the beach. By the faint light of the pre-dawn sky they removed their equipment from the oilskin-wrapped packs and dressed.

Each man pulled on a shirt, patterned in different shades of green and brown. The new French-made *camouflage* clothing was designed to break up the outline of a man, disguising him against a natural backdrop. Like most Imperial officers, Jones had doubted the efficacy of the patterned material – it being somehow typical of the French that they would look to improve the practice of war through the application of fashion. However, witnessing the effective invisibility of an entire squad of French scouts during a training exercise had convinced him of the new cloth's value.

The pair finished their preparations by tucking khaki-coloured trousers into the tops of their boots. "Stops any spiders sneaking up there," joked Kowalski. At least Jones hoped he was joking.

The oilskins that had kept the equipment dry during their swim were folded flat and stuffed into packs bulging with rations and gear. Each man carried a long curved blade, hanging in a sheath from their belts alongside their pistol holsters. In addition, Kowalski had a rifle wrapped in brown burlap, strapped upright to his rucksack.

Pulling his machete from his belt, Jones hacked down a large palm leaf and carried it down to the waterline. He stared out over the waves, trying to discern the shape of the *Neptune*, but could see nothing. The submersible definitely beat any fishing boat when it came to a secret landing. He moved backwards up the beach, brushing the palm fronds across the sand, erasing any tell-tale signs of their arrival. Rejoining Kowalski, he opened his watch and checked the time.

"Dawn won't be long," he said. "Let's get well clear of the beach before anyone's up and about."

The island of Tortuga was a strip of land running east-west, forty miles in length and a dozen in width. A spine of jagged peaks ran down the island's centre, separating the jungles of the northern slopes from the barren scrub of the south. Whilst the northern shores were the more habitable, the island's southern edge boasted the bay of Cayona, a sheltered deep-water anchorage lined with cliffs. This easily-defensible inlet had served as a pirate stronghold for near three hundred years.

Rumour was that under Rackham's leadership, Cayona's natural defences had been bolstered by some formidable man-made additions. Jones planned to find a spot on the ridge overlooking the bay for an initial look, then get down closer for a more detailed inspection.

"We've got to assume they have men stationed on the topmost peaks," said Kowalski. "Let's make sure we don't go running into any of them."

"You're the man with the jungle experience. I'll follow your lead. Time to earn that exorbitant fee of yours Captain."

Jones heard the smile in Kowalski's reply as the pair shouldered their packs. "Heh. You stick close then. And don't go getting bit by anything too poisonous..."

*

Kowalski led them inland through the trees, sometimes skirting the tangled clumps of undergrowth, sometimes hacking a way through, but always heading south and always heading uphill. As the sun's disc climbed above them, the gradient became more evident, and whilst the forest's foliage grew less dense, the steepening incline and the rising temperature kept their progress slower and harder than Jones would have liked.

The Floridian called a halt five hundred feet below the rocky crest of the ridge. He pulled a canteen from his pack, frowning at the sky as he twisted the stopper loose. He took a drink and handed the bottle to Jones.

"I don't like the look of those clouds," he said. "When it rains in these parts, it don't mess around."

"Then the sooner we get up this bloody hill the better."

Jones swigged lukewarm water from the canteen before hoisting his pack once again, waving his hand in an attempt to dispel the cloud of flies buzzing around his head. Perhaps some rain would banish the insects who appeared to have adopted him as a travelling buffet. He slapped at his neck, smearing one of his innumerable tormentors over skin already dotted with itching bites.

They trudged onwards through the thinning trees, the slope becoming steeper still. Jones gasped for breath, leg muscles burning with the effort. Crawling about in the muddy trenches of France for months on end was clearly poor training for a mountain trek, especially in this clammy heat. To Jones' profound irritation, Kowalski seemed to be coping fine with the climb, and appeared oblivious to the flies.

The pair paused in the cover of a boulder, overshadowed by one of the last patches of greenery before the island's bare bones thrust themselves into the sky. Kowalski scanned the ridge ahead through a pair of small binoculars.

"There's some sort of shelter on the peak away to our left," said the Floridian. "But it's set up to watch the sea rather than the slopes, and there are outcrops which will block their view along the ridge once we get up there."

"There's still a fair stretch of open ground to cover from here."

Kowalski gestured to the ominous bank of cloud rolling towards the island on the freshening wind. "Sit tight for half an hour. I reckon we're going to get all the cover we need."

They rested against the rock and ate some of their dry rations as the sun disappeared behind the advancing clouds. The first fat raindrops fell and within moments it was hammering down, bouncing off the rocks and pouring from the tips of the palm fronds above. The initial trickle of water past their feet became a rush of mud as the rain built in intensity. Jones, already soaked through, leaned towards his companion.

"It's bloody tipping it down..."

"Almost as wet as those English summers of yours," said Kowalski. "Come on. Let's move."

Keeping low, they pushed forwards up the hill, shielded from the observers on the mountain peak by the shifting sheets of rain. They struggled up towards the ridge, slipping and sliding, on hands and knees as often as their feet, scrabbling for handholds as the face of the hill liquified under the relentless downpour.

Jones' feet went out from under him, casting him full length on the ground once again. He gave a wry smile as he hauled himself out of the mud for the umpteenth time.

Now this was where his French experience came in handy. He knew all about mud.

*

The slope ended before a sheer wall of rock, rising fifty feet above their heads. The pair stood at the base of the cliff and eyed the obstacle. Jones didn't like the look of the climb, not one bit. The rain might be concealing them from any observers above, but the water was streaming down the rockface, turning what would have been a treacherous enough clamber in fair weather into an almost impossible ascent.

Kowalski squinted up through the downpour. "The ridge runs like this right across the island. The only gap for miles is where Rackham has his men stationed."

"So we climb it here?"

The Floridian shrugged off his backpack. "With a little help from Ramon Cuervo..."

He rummaged in the bag and withdrew the launcher – an ungainly tube of metal, reinforced down its eighteen inch length with hoops of brass. This fat barrel was mounted atop a wooden handgrip studded with dials. As the Floridian began to fiddle with the settings, Jones hunkered down over his own pack and went to work on the projectile.

Twelve inches of gleaming steel, the harpoon flared out at its tip into four viscous barbs. Behind the hooks, the shaft formed an eyelet, through which Jones poked the end of a coil of rope. He pulled it through until he judged the harpoon sat at the line's midpoint, a hundred feet trailing out to either side.

Fearsome needle threaded, he handed the harpoon to Kowalski who slotted it into place and primed the charge. The Floridian raised the launcher in both hands and took aim at the cliff top above.

The pair stood like statues beneath the hammering rain. Water poured down Kowalski's upturned face as his eyes flicked restlessly from one possible anchor point to the next. Jones' trigger finger itched as he watched.

"Whenever you're ready Captain..." he said, unable to restrain his impatience.

Kowalski's brow furrowed, but he didn't divert his attention from the rocks above.

"We only have one more of these spikes Major," he muttered from the side of his mouth. "Reckon you don't really want me to miss."

The launcher barked and the harpoon blasted upwards in a billow of smoke, the loop of rope hauled into the air in its wake. A metallic crack echoed down to them and Kowalski lowered the launcher. He turned to Jones, eyebrow arched.

"Happy now?"

Jones stepped forward and gave the dangling ropes a sharp tug. "Seems solid enough. Here's hoping our chums along the ridge didn't hear anything over the rain."

Kowalski went first, rope tied around his chest. At the base of the cliff, Jones hauled at the other end of the line, arm muscles burning at the effort, hands rubbed raw by the rough fibres of the soaking rope. He frowned up into the rain, convinced his companion could be making more of a contribution to the ascent.

When his own turn came he quickly forgave the Floridian. The rocks were sheer and slick with water, almost devoid of hand- or footholds. It was all he could do to fend himself from the wall as Kowalski hauled him upwards, any attempt at actual climbing lost amidst his efforts to prevent bumps and scrapes turning into more serious blows. It was a relief when he could hook his arm over the protruding shaft of the harpoon and reach up for Kowalski's extended hand. He was pulled, soaked, filthy and aching, over the crest of the ridge.

Jones peered out over the scree and boulders of the slope, searching through the downpour for the outline of the pirate bay away to the south. The torrential rain concealed any details of the shoreline. So much for their elevated observation position.

He began to shiver, the wind against his sodden clothes chilling him now the effort of the climb had passed. He regretted his lack of sou'wester and galoshes – not the first things he'd have put on his list for a trip to a Caribbean island.

"We're going to need to get closer," said Kowalski from alongside him, echoing Jones' own thoughts. "And find some shelter until this muck blows over."

Sitting as much as standing, they slid through the mud and stones of the upper slope down into the boulder field below. A jumble of rocks covered the ground and they had to pick their way carefully down over the haphazard scatter, wary of the narrow gaps between the unstable stones – perfect for the twisting or breaking of an ankle.

At the base of the slope the clutter gave way to an untidy scrubland, dotted with stunted bushes and the occasional outcrop of rock. The barren scenery stretched away to the top of the cliffs, perhaps four miles distant.

They cast about for somewhere to wait out the rain. Neither man fancied moving much closer to the pirate encampment without getting a better look at the lie of the land. In a tall rock formation they discovered a sheltered spot under an overhanging slab of stone. Squeezing in, they sat silently, waiting for the squall to pass.

*

The tropical sun, now high in the sky, warmed the rocks as the rainclouds rolled clear. The whole island steamed as the fallen rain evaporated. To Kowalski, the wreaths of vapour rising up, coupled with the lack of vegetation, made this side of Tortuga look as if it had been newly-decimated by some volcanic eruption. The two men left the shelter of their rock and headed for the cliffs around Cayona, confident the mists curling into the air would mask their approach from any but the most eagle-eyed of watchmen.

Getting closer to their objective, they aimed for a spot where scrappy bushes appeared to overhang the edge of the cliffs, figuring it would provide a concealed position from which to survey the inlet below. They crept forward now, taking turns to move, pistols in hand, the barrel of each weapon fitted with a suppression cylinder, courtesy of Ramon Cuervo. If they did run into any wandering patrols, Kowalski was determined to take care of things quickly, but more importantly, quietly. The thought of rousing the bloodthirsty population of the port and being chased across the island was enough to give him the chills, despite the thick humidity.

With a hundred feet to go, he waved Jones towards the shadow of a large boulder and they slipped their packs from their shoulders. Stashing the bags in a narrow crevice beneath the rock, they crawled forward over the final stretch of broken ground. Jones burrowed in beneath the low branches of the bushes.

Taking a final look around the mist-shrouded cliff top, Kowalski wriggled in after him. Thorns pricked at his face and arms as he pushed his way in. Baked, soaked, and now scratched to pieces in a damned briar patch – Tortuga was proving as welcoming as he had expected.

With a grunt, he pulled free of the clutching barbs and into the hollow beneath the boughs. Jones turned from his position at the crumbling lip of the cliff and waved Kowalski forward.

"Watch you don't knock anything loose."

Kowalski shuffled up alongside the Englishman and peered down over Jack Rackham's stronghold and the waters of Cayona. The cliff walls fell two hundred feet straight down, stretching out right and left of their observation position, enclosing a circular bay perhaps a mile across at its widest point. The southern tips of the cliffs ended in tall spurs of rock facing one another above a narrow stretch of water offering passage out to sea. At their summits Kowalski made out the squat shapes of blockhouses, the slits cut into their walls no doubt offering an expansive field of fire over the waterway below. Beside the bunkers, gun emplacements raised long thin barrels towards the sky. It seemed Rackham was well set to fend off attack from the air as well as the ocean.

Opposite the entrance to the bay, piled untidily against the northern cliffs, sat the town – a shambolic jumble of buildings, not one the twin of its neighbour. Sheds with corrugated iron roofs rubbed up against brick warehouses, whilst tall chimneys leaned over adobe huts and Spanish-style houses. The burnt out shells of buildings stood open to the elements, while other gaps between the tiled roofs were hung with tarpaulins, providing makeshift shelter. Shutters hung askew from stained whitewashed walls and boards covered most of the leaded windows in the sagging wooden frontages along the wharf. Tortuga's three hundred years of undisciplined history could be read in the clash of decaying architecture on display.

A cobbled road traversed its way through the collection of dilapidated buildings. Back and forth it twisted, down the steep slope from clifftop to waterside, serving the triple purpose of thoroughfare, marketplace, and sewer. Down near the waterfront, the street was choked with figures, traders hawking their wares, stevedores laden with bales of cargo, and men rolling barrels between storehouses and the boats moored to the rotting piles of the quay. A clapped-out airship hung over the activity on the wharf, tethered to a wooden tower, its sagging gasbag patched in twenty different shades of filthy canvas.

Tumbledown warehouses sprawled along the base of the cliffs to either side of the town, jetties and wooden docks jutting out into the bay. Off to the east, the smooth surface of the water was broken by the dark shapes of derelict boats, some floating, but most half-submerged, their hulls splintered and broken, a graveyard of ships providing a maritime echo for the ramshackle town.

"Well Major, there it is. Jack Rackham's metropolis."

"Delightful," said Jones, surveying the scene through his eyeglasses. "But I'm more interested in those ships..."

The bay itself was crowded with vessels of all shapes and sizes – fishing boats and steam launches lay at anchor alongside larger rust-streaked tramp steamers. At least a hundred ships were moored below, a mixture of civilian cargo vessels, no doubt engaged in smuggling or other shady dealings, and the outright pirate vessels, plainly armed to the teeth. Amongst them, Kowalski spotted tiny craft fitted with boilers and stubby smokestacks. Little bigger than rowing boats, they seemed almost certain to capsize if they were ever to fire the cannons they sported.

Towering above the ragtag fleet, dominating the bay, was the imposing bulk of a warship. Her rust-streaked hull was four hundred feet long and fifty abeam, her superstructure climbing in tiers from the patched planks of the main deck to a wide bridge flaring out ahead of her three funnels. Four sets of long guns were mounted down her length, and every rail bore the mark of modification as a weapons mounting. The ship fairly bristled with tacked-on armament of all kinds, from hand-cranked Gatling carbines, to swivel-mounted cannons.

Atop it all, reaching up above the smokestacks, was a metal pylon, its criss-cross beams narrowing to a point thirty feet above the bridge. There, fixed at the tower's tip, sat a large brass sphere, its smooth surface gleaming in the sun. Thick cables emerged from its base, snaking down through the girders and into the ship through a hole in the wheelhouse roof.

"What do you think of the contraption up top? Looks electrical."

"Major, you need to keep up with advances in the world of science. That there is an Edison Ball."

Jones turned a baleful look on him. "In my defence, I've had limited opportunity to browse the latest periodicals."

"Heh. Fair enough. Only reason I know is 'cos Maria dragged me to a lecture on the thing last time I was in Boston. Edison himself no less. Can't say I was too impressed. Man's so dull I damn-near fell asleep."

In truth, the only thing preventing him dropping off had been the frequent blows from Maria's sharp elbows. She couldn't comprehend why he hadn't been enthralled, and he couldn't understand why anyone would be. The evening had ended in a fiery row and, eventually, an equally-fiery making-up. Kind of summed-up their relationship.

"Did you stay awake long enough to recall what it does?" asked Jones.

"Not the details, God no. But there was a lot of talk about electric fields and magnetism."

"What do a bunch of pirates want with a bloody magnet?"

Jones frowned at Kowalski's blank look. "Perhaps I should have brought Maria along instead…"

Kowalski returned his gaze to the ship below. "Well whatever that thing does, she's quite the flagship, despite the rust."

"And where the hell did she come from? Your Admiral's estimate of Rackham's strength didn't mention anything along those lines."

"We didn't know a thing about her. Last time any of our boys sneaked a look at this place, Rackham had nothing like that floating around."

"It certainly explains why he suddenly thinks he can go after British shipping with impunity."

Kowalski took a long look at the dreadnought. "Damn it Major. He might be right. That ship down there is as big as anything the Free Fleet has afloat."

"Are you saying your chaps can't do the job?"

Kowalski regarded the collection of pirate vessels. If the whole Fleet rolled out they should be able to handle things down here. But it would get real messy, and the bill would be high – in blood as well as coin.

"We can do it," he said, "but whatever number you were thinking, there's likely an extra nought on the end."

"We'll discuss that later. In fact, I'd rather leave the grubby details of any contract to the penny-pinchers of Whitehall. It's the operational questions I'm concerned with…"

Jones' voice trailed off, both men distracted by the sound of an engine. Below them and off to their right, a launch came into sight between the pillars of rock guarding the entrance to the bay. Jones lifted the glasses and scanned the new arrival as the vessel steamed past their position, heading for the town. The Englishman stiffened, knuckles whitening as his fingers tightened on the binoculars.

"What is it?" asked Kowalski.

Jones handed over the glasses and gestured towards the boat. "Rackham has visitors," he said, his voice hard, matching the look in his eyes.

Kowalski peered down at the launch, running his magnified gaze along the gleaming white trim and spotless planks of the deck. The sun caught the polished brass portholes down her side whilst a cheerful red funnel puffed steam into the air above the honey-varnished wood of her wheelhouse. Nice boat, he thought, definitely not your average pirate vessel.

Standing at the launch's stern were two figures. The first bore the unmistakeable features of Rook, sunlight bouncing off his metallic skull. Alongside him, hands on the rail, staring out at the surrounding ships, was the ample frame of Commodore Silas Culpepper of the United States Navy.

*

"I've stolen my fair share of things in my time Major – a train, even an airship once. But laundry? This is a first." The Floridian peered doubtfully at the threadbare garments they had liberated from the washing line.

"At least it's clean," replied Jones, removing his shirt and tugging a rough denim one on in its place. He sniffed at the cloth as he buttoned it up. "Well, cleanish."

The sight of Culpepper in the stern of the launch had changed the nature of the mission. A reconnaissance of Cayona was no longer enough. Jones needed to know what was going on, and he wasn't going to get any answers perched on a clifftop. They would have to take a stroll into town.

With the volume of shipping in the bay, and the amount of trade going on, they reckoned a couple of new faces would pass unremarked. Their *camouflage* shirts however, were quite another matter, and it had been a relief when they came across the drying line before penetrating too far into the jumble of narrow streets. Unpegging a shirt or two certainly bested the original plan of clubbing someone over the head and stealing their garments – a risky undertaking at the best of times.

Knocking an adversary unconscious always left the thorny problem of them eventually coming round and raising the alarm. There was an easy solution for such a dilemma of course, but it seemed disproportionate to kill a man in cold blood simply because you wanted to borrow his outfit – unsporting somehow. Besides, as Kowalski had observed, the shirt from the fellow you had to thump on the skull invariably turned out to be too small, or came in a dreadfully unfashionable check. Looting the washing line, with its choice of size and style, had been like an appointment with a Savile Row tailor in comparison.

Now, clad in still-damp stolen garb, the pair stepped out of the shelter of the alleyway and onto the main street running down the hillside towards the waters of the bay.

At first there were few signs of life, and fewer still of any activity – the odd drunk slumbering in a doorway, the occasional scrawny child chasing after an equally thin and dirty dog. But as they descended, the hustle and bustle grew – stalls lining the roadside, compressing the pedestrian traffic inward. Their progress down the hill became a torturous dance, attention divided between negotiating their passage through the crowd, sidestepping the sewer channel running the centre of the street, and avoiding eye contact with the stallholders, beggars and doxies, all desperate for an opening to make their pitch for coin.

Whilst most of the hawking and bartering was being carried out in English, the pronunciation and accents Jones picked out ran the gamut from impeccable to near-incomprehensible. The variety of voices was reflected in the faces of the crowd. It seemed every race and nation was represented on Tortuga – the mercantile low-life of the world, attracted by the promise of unfettered commerce and illicit opportunity.

Eventually the street met the square, and the press of people thinned as it flowed outward. The stalls gave way to shops and taverns, their ancient wooden frames leaning drunkenly against one another, surrounding three sides of the wide cobbled space bordering the waterfront. Jones headed for the centre of the square, Kowalski doing his best nonchalant stroll alongside him. They stopped before a cart piled high with fruit and vegetables, taking turns to browse the wares whilst the other had a look around.

"Busy place," said Kowalski, his voice low. "If Rackham's getting a cut of all this, he must be doing well for himself."

Jones lifted an apple and turned it over, examining it for bruises. "And he's keeping a close eye on things. Making sure he gets his share. Two men on the roof of the pub on the corner. Another two by the wharf."

"You see the cannons? At least three of them, covering the jetties. Reckon you don't cause any trouble in Calico Jack's town. Not if you want to leave in one piece."

Jones tossed the apple to Kowalski and picked up another. He gestured over his shoulder with his thumb. "And if they don't pop a round into your boat, they stretch your neck..."

At the edge of the square stood a raised wooden platform, a scaffold looming above. Hanging from the crossbeam was a body, face swollen and black above the noose digging into its neck.

Jones pulled a coin from his pocket and handed over payment for the fruit. "What did he do?" he asked the stallholder, indicating the dangling corpse.

The man shrugged. "Feller beat up a strumpet."

"One of Jack's favourites? Must have been if he cared enough to hang him."

"Don't reckon so. Doubt Jack gives a damn about the bint. Ways I heard it, the feller thought he could beat her up without paying for it." The stallholder turned away to deal with another customer.

"Delightful," muttered Jones as they moved off.

The pair paused in the shadow of the wooden tower acting as a mooring point for the airship tethered above. The haphazard timber frame looked less than robust, unlikely to provide much security in the event of the wind getting up. But in fairness, the rickety structure was a good match for the airship's battered gondola and threadbare balloon. The decrepit craft made for quite a contrast with the luxurious dirigible in which Jones had soared across the Atlantic.

Jones gestured toward another pylon of criss-crossed beams rising amongst the chimneys over the town, this one topped with a tall metal rod.

"Wireless tower," he said. "Our pirate chums appear to enjoy all the modern conveniences."

Kowalski turned towards him, eyes wide. "Wireless..."

"What about it?"

"I know why Rackham has an Edison Ball..."

"Feel free to enlighten me."

"The lecture – Edison kept droning on about reducing unwanted effects..."

"If you have a point to this story, now would be the time to reveal it."

"The magnetism – it blocks radio waves. The bigger the ball, the bigger the effect."

They both turned to regard the dreadnought and the brass sphere catching the sunlight high above her decks. Knowledge of the ship's invisible power over the airwaves only served to increase the sense of menace she radiated. Jones imagined all the distress calls, tapped out by desperate wireless operators, gobbled up by magnetic disturbance, never to reach a friendly ear.

"Enough sightseeing," he said. "Time to find out what Rackham and Culpepper are up to."

"I know the best place for gossip in most ports. I imagine Cayona ain't any different."

The two men turned their attention to the largest of the taverns.

"A little early for whisky..." said Jones.

"Heh. Rum it is then."

Jones rubbed the apple on his sleeve, taking a bite as they crossed the square. He'd missed lunch, and rum on an empty stomach was never a good idea.

*

The pub's tables were as dirty as its floor, and the air was thick with the stench of cheap drink and stale sweat. The service matched the ambience, their only welcome a sullen stare from an ugly barman as he poured their drinks. The place was everything Jones had expected, a grim dive of a tavern. Naturally, it was packed.

He and Kowalski stood pressed against the counter, nervous of their elbows lest they spill someone's drink and get embroiled in a fight. Jostled by the crowd, they lifted their rum, Jones wincing at the gutrot smell of the dark brown liquid. The taste was quite as awful as the aroma promised. As he lowered his hand, he tipped most of the drink onto the floor. The stuff would likely burn a hole in the planks, but better the floor than his innards.

He kept his ears cocked for anything interesting, but the only snatches of conversation he could catch were slurred arguments over favourite ports, favourite pubs, even favourite knots. Sailors' drunken chatter was nothing if not predictable. One robust discussion regarding favourite songs broke out into a competitive, simultaneous rendition of the verses in question. Within moments, the entire pub was engaged, either in tuneless support of one or other of the ditties, or in loud demands for the singers to cease their caterwauling.

Jones leaned toward his companion. "This is hopeless. Let's get out of here."

He straightened, ready to leave, but was brought up short as Kowalski's hand gripped his arm.

"Don't go rushing off," said the Floridian, his eyes fixed over Jones' shoulder. "I just spotted someone we'll want to talk to..."

Kowalski pushed his way through the crowd and over to one of the booths set around the walls, Jones following behind. The seats held a solitary drinker, head bowed over a glass and bottle, both empty. The Floridian slipped onto the bench alongside the slumped figure and Jones took the seat opposite.

The head came up slowly, bleary eyes struggling to focus, widening as the man's rum-soaked brain processed the identities of his new companions. The mouth dropped open in shock, revealing a flash of gold.

"Hello Luis," said Kowalski. "You owe us two hundred dollars."

*

Jones tightened the rope around Luis' wrists and pushed a wad of dirty rags into the Cuban's mouth, muffling his protests. Another strip of the same oil-stained cloth secured the gag in place. The Englishman straightened up from the prone figure and Kowalski tucked his pistol away, no longer worried about their reluctant guide making a bid for freedom.

In the alley behind the tavern, Kowalski had forced Luis to his knees and pushed the fat brass barrel of the silenced pistol between the Cuban's gold teeth. Luis' eyes had darted between the men standing over him, brimming with terrified tears as Kowalski explained in lurid detail what would happen if he didn't help them get a closer look at Jack Rackham's operations.

There had been a flash of hope as Luis caught movement in his peripheral vision – a scullery maid from the tavern lugging a slop bucket out into the alleyway. She had taken a long look at the frozen tableau before her, taking in the kneeling man and the gun before dropping her gaze, pouring the bucket's contents into the hard-packed earth and turning away. With what Kowalski had seen of Tortuga, he reckoned it wasn't the first such scene the girl had witnessed.

With the maid's silent departure, the last thin thread of Luis' courage snapped. He had begged, agreeing to do whatever they wanted, desperate words distorted, made almost incoherent by the gun between his teeth.

They had made their way through the backstreets of Cayona, Kowalski clutching Luis' arm, pistol shoved into the man's side. Away from the square and main street there were few people about, and those few who passed didn't pay the trio a blind bit of notice as they made their way to the docks.

Luis' boat was twenty feet in length, with a raised wheelhouse towards the bow and an open deck astern surrounded by a low rail. Her timbers were patched everywhere with different kinds of wood and streaked with a variety of paints. A single rusted smokestack poked upwards from the centre of the decking, the dented metal held upright in a web of guy lines. Quite the bucket, thought Kowalski.

Jones had shrugged, indicating their captive. "He made it here from Havana. She must be reasonably watertight."

Once aboard, they slipped the mooring and steamed out into the bay. They picked their way through the crowded anchorage, course roughly parallel to the shore, Kowalski careful to ensure Luis didn't take them too close to any of the larger pirate vessels. Ahead of them, glowing in the light of the evening sun, the cliffs reared up and around, forming an imposing backdrop beyond the battered shipwrecks.

Out at the far edge of town, a large brick-built warehouse stood apart from the others, a wooden jetty protruding into the bay from the broad doors set into its frontage. Despite its proximity to the maritime graveyard, the building and its dock were in considerably better repair than the other structures along Cayona's crumbling waterfront. That, and the sleek lines of the pristine steam launch moored at the pier, suggested the building belonged to Rackham.

"That is the place," Luis had confirmed, cutting the throttle on the engine, allowing the boat to coast to a halt on the calm water, drifting in close to one of the derelict hulks. The Cuban had flatly refused to go any closer in – his terror of Rackham and the consequences of treachery finally overwhelming his fear of Kowalski's pistol.

So now Luis lay trussed up on his thin cot in the compartment below the wheelhouse as Jones and Kowalski waited for evening. Under cover of darkness they would slip in closer and see if they couldn't take a look at Calico Jack's warehouse, before making for the northern shore and their rendezvous with Brunel.

*

Beneath the high cliffs, darkness fell across the bay with a startling abruptness. Away to their left the lights of the town reflected in the water, but as the daytime bustle of the waterfront petered out, only isolated pools of flickering gaslight punctuated the gloom around Rackham's warehouse. Their boat floated a hundred yards from the end of the wooden jetty. An easy swim, a creep along the pier, and then we shall see what we shall see, thought Jones. He tapped Kowalski on the shoulder – time to go.

The two men rose, ready to slip over the side, only to duck back into shadow as bright electric lamps crackled into life down the length of the pier, one after the other, their harsh white light shattering the blackness. With a rumble the warehouse doors slid open on their runners and a dozen men came out onto the dock.

"What's all this about?" whispered Jones, peering from the cover of the rail towards the sudden burst of activity.

Kowalski tugged at his sleeve and nodded in the direction of the bay. There, moving towards them over the water was the dark outline of a trawler, running in without lights. The throb of its engine reached their ears, the wake of its passage causing their boat to pitch to and fro. The noise died away as the new arrival approached the pier, low greetings called out and answered with tossed ropes. The vessel was hauled in by the waiting men, bumping against the wooden pilings as it was tied up alongside Culpepper's launch.

The fishing boat's crew began hauling sacks up from the hold, passing them in a chain from one man to the next, down the gangway and onto the jetty. The assembled dock workers took charge of the cargo, stacking it up on wheeled carts.

Kowalski gave him another nudge. "We're not the only observers..."

Beyond the activity on the pier, standing in the wide doorway of the warehouse, were two figures. Even at a distance, Jones recognised the rotund build of Culpepper.

"The other one. Rackham?"

"Yep. That's him."

Jones rummaged in his pack and pulled the binoculars free. He raised the glasses and adjusted the optics, bringing Calico Jack Rackham into sharp focus. The pirate was taller than Culpepper, and thinner, his sharp features cast into stark relief by the lights – dark hair swept back from a high forehead, the brows casting deep pools of shadow on either side of a hook nose.

Too far away, thought Jones. He needed to be closer – needed to see the man's eyes. His hands tightened into fists at the thought of a more personal confrontation with his brother's murderer.

"Shame I left the rifle under that rock," said Kowalski. "Two bullets and I could have saved you and Buckingham a whole heap of cash."

"I'd give you Culpepper," said Jones. "But I'm old-fashioned enough to want to deal with Rackham myself. Besides, I need to know what's going on, and dead men tell no tales, as I'm sure these characters would put it."

"So you still want to go take a look?"

"More than ever. I'm intrigued now. What sort of cargo is so important the King of the Pirates and the bloody overlord of Cuba feel the need to personally oversee its unloading?"

The Floridian eyed the stretch of water between the boat and the jetty, the glare from the electric lamps washing over the surface.

"A little bright out there, Major." He gestured to their right where the upturned boats and rusting shipwrecks cast patches of dark shadow. "We might want to take the long way around."

The swim took them a good twenty minutes, the pace slow and steady, strokes kept carefully beneath the surface to minimise any noise or tell-tale splashes that might catch the light. They hauled themselves up onto the rocks two hundred yards along the shore from the warehouse. Out here, beyond the edge of town, they were sure nobody would see them clamber out of the water. All the same, they moved quickly, keeping low, ensuring they found a sheltered niche amongst the stones before pausing. Both men lifted the footwear which hung from tied laces over their shoulders, tipped out the water, and slipped their feet into damp boots.

Jones grimaced at the unpleasant sensation. "Wouldn't that be just the thing?" he whispered. "Spend a year crawling around in the mud in France, only to get trench foot here."

"Heh. Tropical island life not living up to expectations?"

Kowalski slid an oilskin package out from where it had nestled in the small of his back, unwrapping their silenced pistols and handing one across.

Jones took the weapon and regarded the dark bulk of the warehouse silhouetted against the lights of the pier. "Shall we?"

*

Luis jerked out of his exhausted doze as something bumped and scraped down the side of the boat. The oily taste of the rag clogging his mouth made him gag for the hundredth time, but with an effort he resisted the urge to retch. With the balled up rag and the tight strip around his lower face, throwing up would be the end of him.

He flexed his cramping limbs once more, wincing as the movement caused the ropes at his wrists and ankles to chafe. When his captors had left, he had squirmed against his restraints, but earned himself nothing but raw patches of skin. Anger and fear burned through him as he blinked tears in the darkness. Bound and gagged – a prisoner on his own boat.

His vessel rocked as someone clambered aboard. Those gringo bastards were back. They would sail out of the bay and dump him overboard. Send down a trussed-up meal for the sharks. He was sure of it – it was what he would have done himself.

He heard footsteps in the wheelhouse above, and then voices. Strangers' voices, he realised with a sudden surge of hope.

"Nobody around..." said the first voice.

"Check below," answered another. "She shouldn't be out here. Locals know better than to moor in this part of the bay."

Luis wriggled around in the confines of his cot, straining to see as footsteps clattered down the wooden ladder. The door swung open and a figure stood in the companionway, lantern held aloft, the light flooding into the tiny sleeping compartment. Luis blinked up at his saviour and tried to speak.

The man ignored the muffled begging and called over his shoulder. "There's a bloke down 'ere..."

More footsteps, and the shape of another figure behind the lantern.

"Well, well," said the new arrival. "If it ain't my old pal Luis."

The first man stepped aside and Rook squeezed past him into the cabin. The bloodshot eye stared down and Luis' pleas choked in his throat. He'd sooner have faced the sharks.

"Now matey, I'm going to give you a moment," said Rook, leaning forward, bringing his ruined face down to loom scant inches from Luis' own. "I want you to have a good hard think about the story you'll be telling old Rooky when I haul that there plug out of your mouth..."

*

Jack Rackham watched his men wheel the last of the sacks into the warehouse. He took a final draw on his cigarette and flicked the butt out over the jetty's rail. The ember glowed red as it flew its arc, before snuffing out abruptly in the dark water below. Rackham nodded to the guards and stepped over the threshold. The wooden doors rumbled shut behind him.

Crates and barrels rose up on either side in haphazard towers as he made his way through the warehouse, the contraband haul of a hundred raids and smuggling trips. Deep pools of cobweb-strung shadow filled the gaps between the stacks and the air was thick with the smell of damp and dust. Only at the building's centre was there any open space. Here, a single electrical lamp hung down on a long chain from the ceiling, casting a sickly illumination over the newly-arrived cargo and the portly figure engaged in its inspection.

Culpepper – checking up on him again. Still, business was business. Rackham fixed a smile in place, time to play the jolly trader.

"Everything to your satisfaction Commodore?"

The American straightened. "It all appears to be in order. The quantities are as agreed."

Rackham reached out and patted a hand on the topmost of the hessian bags. "All ready for refining. Bolivia's finest – as promised."

"As paid for," corrected Culpepper.

Rackham maintained his smile with an effort. "And the other matter? Mister Rook's work proved up to scratch?"

Culpepper glanced round at mention of the Irishman, seeking for his distinctive features and displaying visible relief at their absence. Rook made people nervous. It was the reason Rackham kept him around. Nothing ensured your business partners remained honest like having a pet lunatic at your beck and call.

"Your men completed their task admirably," said Culpepper. "I received another delegation yesterday. More villagers begging for protection. One more month and I shall give them what they ask. My soldiers will move into the villages and, as if by magic," an unpleasant smirk formed beneath the moustache, "the bandit raids shall cease."

"Making you look quite the hero..."

"And Estrada quite the fool. His pathetic insurgency will have lost all credibility and support. Cuba will be pacified, and all without my men having fired a single shot."

"Although mine will have surely fired plenty on their behalf," said Rackham. It did no harm to remind the Commodore his hands were clean only because others' were stained crimson, right up to the wrists.

"A job for which you have been handsomely rewarded," snapped Culpepper, the whiskered cheeks flushing red. Not for the first time, Rackham thought how much he'd enjoy playing the American at cards – the man's podgy face was like an open book.

"And there you go again," he said. "Treating me like I'm the hired help, rather than a full-share partner in this here enterprise."

"You have your ship. And now you have your instructions. The cargo needs to be in New Orleans tomorrow evening."

"Deauchamp's boys are expecting it?"

"Yes," sniffed the American, mouth wrinkled in disapproval. "The negro will be awaiting delivery."

Rackham snorted. "I do so feel for your delicate sensibilities Commodore. Forced into associating with unsavoury characters like myself, and now, Heaven forbid, negroes?" He indicated the pile of sacks. "And all in the honourable endeavour of flooding your own country with cocaine."

Culpepper drew himself up, affronted, puffing out his chest until it almost matched the girth of his stomach. "My country? My country fell at Appomattox."

Rackham smiled. "You can't have been much more than an itch in your daddy's britches when Lee surrendered..."

"My father died fighting the Yankees. The Stars and Stripes is nothing to me but a flag of convenience. Besides, we're hardly flooding the country, as you rather dramatically put it." He nodded towards the stacked cargo. "Somebody has to supply this filth to the degenerates who choose to use it."

"And somebody has to make a pretty profit doing it..."

"For the moment." Culpepper's eyes narrowed. "But like the raids on the Cuban villages, all this is the means to an end. Suppression of the cocaine trade will be one of my first successes when I am ensconced within the White House."

*

At mention of the American seat of government, Jones and Kowalski shared a troubled look. From their concealed position amongst the crates, the infiltrators had eavesdropped on the conversation with an increasing sense of disquiet. In the minutes since Jones had put a silenced round through the padlock on the warehouse's rear door, their simple reconnaissance mission had spiralled downwards into a dark morass of murder, illicit substances, and political conspiracy.

Jones' mind churned, torn as to the course of action to pursue. Should he relay this new information to Buckingham, and let the top brass back home decide what to do? Or might he end things here and now?

Staring out of the darkness at his brother's murderer, Jones knew he had no choice at all. The old men in the comfortable offices of Whitehall might be put out at a lack of consultation, but Jones couldn't let an opportunity like this slip through his fingers. Then again, perhaps Buckingham and his cronies would be pleased? After all, a handful of bullets would prove a damn sight cheaper than hiring the whole Free Fleet.

He looked to Kowalski and tilted his head towards the pair in the centre of the warehouse. The usual playful glint in the Floridian's eyes was absent, replaced by a steely look, a match to Jones' own. The business of killing was at hand, and both men settled into a hard, ruthless professionalism.

"Well mateys, what do we have here?"

They whirled, hands reaching for weapons, but pulling up short when presented with the sight of Rook, squatting atop the crate at their rear, a pistol in each hand, the lower half of his face stretched into a skeleton grin.

"Mister Jones of The London Times, unless I am very much mistaken. And here I thought my old mate Luis had to be lying." He lifted his head and called out. "Jack, we've got visitors."

The conversation at the centre of the warehouse came to a sudden halt. Rook gestured towards the light with the wave of a pistol.

"Let's go see Captain Rackham, shall we?"

*

The infiltrators knelt on the rough planks of the warehouse floor, relieved of their weapons, hands lifted to the backs of their heads, an armed sailor covering them from behind. Rackham ignored the captives for the moment, seemingly more interested in rummaging through their equipment, piled atop a barrel. It was Culpepper who spoke first.

"This is an unwelcome surprise. I had understood from Captain Rackham's associate that you would be leaving the Caribbean at the earliest opportunity. You appear determined to stick your nose in where it's not required."

"In truth, the threats only made me more interested," answered Jones. If Culpepper was still swallowing his cover as a reporter, Jones wasn't about to put him right.

"And now you've stumbled on a bigger story than you imagined. I assume you've been lurking back there for some time."

"Long enough," shrugged Jones.

"A pity."

"Don't want your sordid little scheme revealed to the world? Peddling cocaine – not the behaviour one expects from a military man."

It was Culpepper's turn to shrug. "Election campaigns are expensive."

"So you're going to buy the Presidency?"

"Not at all. I shall simply use the money to better inform the populace regarding my suitability for the post." The American gave a smile. "The masses do so love a war hero."

The noise of the door scraping open brought a halt to the discussion, Culpepper falling silent as Luis stumbled into the warehouse's centre, pushed forward by Rook into the circle of light. Rackham turned from his perusal of the equipment to face the new arrival.

"Luis, my old friend," said the pirate, wagging a finger at the Cuban. "Seems you've been running a passenger service."

The sailor rubbed at his wrists and shot the captives a venomous glance.

"These men *senor*, they kidnap Luis. They steal his boat and force him to –"

"Save your breath," said Rackham. "I don't care."

The pirate raised the weapon he'd pulled from the pile. Luis' face turned grey at the sight of the gaping muzzle. A hollow boom echoed around the warehouse and the Cuban staggered, clutching his stomach, coughing out ragged breaths, scrabbling with his fingers at the steel bolt protruding from his guts. Rackham put the launcher down and reached for one of the silenced pistols, ignoring the harpooned sailor's moans.

He raised the gun, waving it before Luis' eyes, before adopting a theatrical duelling stance, arm straight, turned side-on, squinting along the barrel at the wounded man. Luis stared up, tears streaming down his face. The gun spat, the report little more than a muffled pop, the noise of the bullet's sickening smack almost as loud. Luis dropped like a stone, a neat red hole in his forehead.

Ignoring the fallen man, Rackham turned the pistol this way and that, admiring the shining brass of the suppression cylinder.

"Nice gun. And quite the arsenal for a journalist." He tossed the pistol aside and turned to look at the kneeling men. "I'm not buying this story of yours. Not for a moment." He waved a hand dismissively at Kowalski. "This one we know. A gun for hire –"

"Much like yourself..." said the Floridian.

Rackham paused, an eyebrow raised at the interruption. He peered down his sharp nose at Kowalski before lifting his gaze to Rook.

The Irishman's kick caught Kowalski in the back, pitching him forward, smashing his face into the floor. Immediately Rook was on him, knee between the shoulder blades, pulling his head up by a fistful of hair, pressing the muzzle of his gun to the captive's temple.

"Now matey, you don't want to be giving any cheek to the Captain..." He rapped the pistol hard against Kowalski's skull. "Behave yourself."

Rook stood and the Floridian pulled himself back to his knees. Rackham stepped forward, looming over Jones.

"As I was saying, before your friend's interjection, something don't smell right in this here tale. Not right at all. You've gone to quite some lengths for a newspaper story..."

Jones stared up. Silent. Defiant.

The pirate beckoned Rook forward and put an arm around his subordinate's shoulders. He reached up his other hand and beat a tattoo with his knuckles on the metal plating of the Irishman's head. "I'm thinking maybe I should let Mister Rook indulge his passion for knifework. See if he can't winkle the truth out of you –"

"Ask him about his brother," muttered Kowalski, prompting everyone to turn in his direction.

The Floridian lifted his head to meet Jones' accusatory gaze. "Don't look at me like that," he said. "Easier this way than trying to keep your secrets..."

Rackham's eyes gleamed as he took in this exchange. "Your mercenary friend is wise beyond his years. Secrets is it? What's all this about a brother?"

Jones knew Kowalski was right. Let Rackham and Culpepper think they had uncovered the truth, disguising the greater secret of his real identity and mission. All the same, nothing was feigned about the bitterness in his voice. "He was the skipper of the *Milford*."

Rackham grinned at this revelation, but Culpepper was mystified. "What is he talking about?"

"A merchant tub we took weeks past," answered the pirate. "Nice haul of weapons aboard. And she made excellent practice for the gunners."

Jones could feel his anger burning in his face. Rackham saw it and gave a slow nod.

"That's more like it. That's a tale I can swallow." He turned to Culpepper. "I think we've found out what really motivates our friend here..."

Looking down again, the pirate's eyes bored into Jones' own.

"Vengeance," said Rackham, relishing the word. "Now there's a cause worth dying for."

*

Kowalski splashed into the water off the bottom of the ladder, ripples spreading out over the oily surface, illuminated by the faint light from the shaft mouth twenty feet above.

The Pit – so Rackham had named it as he had given Rook his orders. The Irishman had summoned a couple of burly cronies to act as guards and the captives had been marched through Tortuga's dark alleyways to a courtyard off the town's central square. There, the pirates manhandled a heavy trapdoor up and back, revealing the gaping maw of a shaft set into the cobbles.

The footing was rough beneath the waist-high water as Kowalski stepped away from the brick wall towards the pool's centre. Looking up he saw Jones picking his way down the rungs, followed by one of their escorts. Beyond the descending figures, he could make out Rook's distinctive features grinning down, his leer given a demonic cast by the flickering orange flame of the lantern he held up over the pit's circular opening.

Jones dropped from the lowest rung and into the water, joined moments later by their guard. The pirate grunted, shoving them towards the centre of the pool, apparently confident the prisoners would comply. A fair assumption, granted Kowalski, seeing as Rook's companion at the top of the shaft was covering them with a formidable blunderbuss.

Pushed back to back, they stood in silence as their captor bent low, fumbling in the water at their feet. Kowalski felt cold metal clasp his ankle, then his foot was pulled roughly to the surface, almost tipping him over. The pirate attached a padlock to the shackle and released the leg, allowing Kowalski to regain his balance. Grunting once more, the man turned to perform the same procedure on Jones. Task complete, their taciturn jailer clambered up the ladder to rejoin his fellows above.

Kowalski bent down, feeling out the manacle, following the chain to a ring fixed in the shaft floor. He gave the anchor point an experimental tug, to no effect.

"Ahoy there..." called Rook, his voice reverberating down. "Accommodation to your satisfaction?"

"Just dandy thank you," shouted Kowalski, damned if he'd let the man's taunting get to him. Well, not so as the bastard would notice.

"You're a couple of characters, I'll grant you that," came the response. "But I predict there'll be a mite less banter when we come for you in the morning." The Irishman laughed, the noise bouncing off the walls. "You'll be looking forward to the noose by then. Likely arguing over who gets to die first."

The prisoners stood in the water, staring upwards as Rook turned away and the trapdoor was dropped into place. Its timbers smashed like thunder against the cobbles, sealing them in.

*

A thick, choking blackness closed around the two men at the bottom of the shaft. Deprived of sight, Jones found himself disoriented, staggering in the darkness, turning this way and that, desperate for a hint of light. When Kowalski spoke it was a relief to have something to focus on.

"Least they let us climb down. I wouldn't have put it past that freak to have just tossed us in."

"And risk upsetting whatever his master has planned? Not likely. Rook's a nasty piece of work, but I do believe even he is more than a little afraid of Rackham."

"Well if he ain't, he's even crazier than I thought."

"Shall we explore our lodgings?" suggested Jones.

The two men shuffled outwards as far as their restraints would allow. From there they reached out, leaning forward until fingertips brushed against the slimy brickwork of their watery prison. They ran their hands over every inch of wall within reach, finding nothing of note but the rusting steps of the ladder – a tantalising offer of escape, denied to them by their iron tethers. A similar fumbling search of the uneven stone beneath the water yielded the same result, nothing to help their predicament. Straightening up, Jones made an unpleasant discovery.

"The water is rising. Either that or my legs have shrunk." He lifted his fingers to his lips then spat away into the blackness. "Salt water. This bloody hole is connected to the sea."

"This gets better and better, don't it?" Kowalski's tired voice came out of the dark. "High tide was around three, when we'd arranged to meet Brunel. Think we're lucky enough that this is as deep as it gets?"

Jones shrugged and shook his head, before realising his companion could see neither gesture in the Stygian darkness. "I've lost track of time somewhat since our chums relieved me of my watch, but it's probably only ten o'clock or so." He gave a bitter laugh. "That watch was my father's. Bloody good one too. Doubt I'll be seeing it again anytime soon."

"We get out of here? I'll buy you a new one. One of Ramon's finest."

"I'll hold you to that. However, I think we may have some swimming to do before then..."

The water level crept inexorably higher as time ground past. They stood for as long as they could, up on tiptoes, necks craned back, until they were forced to bow to the inevitable. They slipped their boots from their feet and began to tread water.

At first the motion was almost relaxing, Jones able to ignore the drag of the chain on his ankle. Deprived of light, with arms and legs stirring the warm water in slow, hypnotic circles, his mind wandered. Memories of his earliest trips out on the Solent filled his head – he and his brother, stuffed into bulky cork lifejackets in the stern of the sailing boat, listening in earnest attention as their father delivered instruction on what to do if they were stupid enough to fall over the side.

"Don't fight the current. Don't fight the sea. You can't win. Save your energy for shouting." He and Michael had stared wide-eyed at each other, then back to their father. "Don't try and make for the boat. You'll tire yourself out. Let the boat come for you."

No boat coming for you here old chap, he thought, a grumbling ache beginning to manifest itself in his muscles. Just as no boat had come for Michael.

The pain slowly grew in intensity, pushing memories from his head, beginning to dominate his thoughts. He and Kowalski shared the occasional grunt of acknowledgement as tired limbs bumped against one another, but mostly they remained silent, concentrating on the simple, immediate task of staying afloat.

A stabbing agony of cramp seized Jones' leg and he cried out, clutching at his thigh before slipping beneath the surface, shackle and sodden clothing dragging him down. He panicked, gulping a mouthful of brine before he felt hands pulling him upwards. He was turned, held up from behind as he coughed and retched. Kowalski's legs flailed beneath them, struggling to keep both men above the water.

Jones stretched his leg out straight, desperate to get the knotted tendons working again. Eventually the vice-like grip of the cramp loosened and he was able to move once more.

"Thanks," he croaked into the blackness.

"Don't mention it," came the weary reply. "Reckon you'll be returning the favour before too long."

Kowalski's prediction proved accurate as the hours stretched out in a dark haze of aches and cramps, each man forced to help as the other floundered. Jones' entire world narrowed into a single purpose, keeping his leaden limbs in motion and his face out of the water.

The first time his foot scraped on rock the significance passed him by – the blow just another addition to his variety of pains. But at the second occurrence, his exhausted brain figured it out. He stopped the rotation of his legs and straightened them, the muscles screaming in protest. His toes discovered the bottom of the shaft and he stood, head clear of the water.

Kowalski's groan of relief sounded a moment later, indicating he too had found solid ground beneath his feet. "Thank Christ," breathed the Floridian.

"Amen to that," answered Jones.

They stood in the darkness, leaning against one another, all energy spent, silent as the water ebbed away. Eventually able to sit, they slumped down, tortured leg muscles finally ceasing their trembling. Sitting quietly in the dark, aching in every joint, Jones fell into a fitful slumber.

The next thing he knew he was jerked into wakefulness, strong hands grabbing at him and lifting him up. The pirates had come for him.

*

The rough hemp fibres scraped over Jones' face as Rook pulled the noose down. The pirate waved a hand and the line was hauled taut, biting into Jones' neck, hoisting him up onto his toes.

Rook shoved him round, checking the knots binding his hands and feet before spinning him back to face the crowd of cutthroats gathered in the square. The Irishman pushed his ravaged face right up against Jones', his lidless eye gleaming.

"Don't you be running off now matey."

He grabbed a hessian bag from where it hung over the wooden railing and lifted it towards Jones' head. Rackham stopped him.

"No hood. I want to see his face."

The Irishman shrugged and moved away, crossing the platform to stand at Rackham's shoulder as the pirate leader addressed the men standing below.

"Brethren of the Coast!" shouted Rackham. "I have a question to place before the assembly. A question of justice." He waved a hand towards Jones. "This here visitor to our fine shores claims to be a reporter. For the London Times, no less. Now I know you all to be erudite and well-read gentlemen..." This drew a ripple of laughter. "So you may be of a mind to let the pen-pusher go?"

A stony silence followed this remark and Rackham turned with a look of mock concern. "It's not looking too good here mate," he said in a stage whisper, drawing another laugh from the crowd.

Jones would have loved to cast back some witty retort, but the effort of balancing on tiptoe was beginning to tell. All his focus was set on ignoring the ache in his calves, his muscles reminding him of their efforts in the pit during the night. If Rackham was going to hang him, then he might at least cut out the bloody speeches and get on with it.

"On the other hand," called the pirate, continuing the charade, "perhaps you fine fellows are of a private disposition and object to gentlemen of the press prying into your affairs?"

A chorus of agreement sounded out. "That's right Jack, I hate bein' in the society pages," cried one wag.

Rackham echoed the general laughter. "My sentiments exactly. I'd prefer the great unwashed didn't hear about all the fancy parties we're attending." His voice rose. "In fact, I don't want the English knowing a damned thing about us. Not until we've picked off every last one of those juicy supply ships. Then, when we're good and ready, we'll kick them out of the Caribbean for good."

Shouting now above the cheers of his men, Rackham continued, gesturing out towards the rusting dreadnought dominating the bay. "And now we've got the ship to do it. What say you lads? Shall we use her to give those English bastards a front page or two worth reading?"

The gathered pirates roared their agreement and Rackham's eyes shone. He waited for the cheers to die down and then raised his hand to point at Jones.

"But before we get started on that enjoyable task, let's be dealing with this here piece of flotsam." He adopted a solemn expression and lowered his voice, forcing the assembled crowd to lean forward, intent on his every word. "By the powers vested in me, as appointed Captain of these here Brethren, I do hereby sentence this man to be hanged by the neck..." he made a theatrical pause and gave Jones a wink "...until dead."

Once again the cheers rang out and Rackham revelled in the noise and approval, nodding his appreciation as he crossed the platform to stand before Jones. The pirate raised a finger and prodded Jones in the chest, pushing him off balance, forcing him to make little hops on his bound feet to maintain his balance. Muscles complaining as the crowd hooted with cruel laughter, Jones decided he'd had quite enough of being a prop in Jack Rackham's cabaret.

"Get on with it," he said.

Rackham's smile turned feral and he raised his hand. "Say hello to your brother..."

But the signal didn't come. Instead, the pirate leader was ducking for cover along with his men as an explosion rocked the square, the air suddenly filled with noise and a hail of splinters.

Ears ringing, Jones hopped round, straining to see the source of the blast. The smouldering remains of a trawler floated beside the quay, its upper deck twisted and blackened, flames licking up from its exposed innards. A lazy ball of smoke rolled high into the air above the wreckage as dazed men picked themselves up along the length of the waterfront.

The boat's hull shifted, shunted upwards as something struck it from below – something massive. The onlookers backed away from the quay as the water boiled, a dark shape rising beneath the turbulence. The nervousness in the crowd turned to naked terror as the mechanical beast tore through the floating debris and burst to the surface.

The *Neptune* surged forward, smashing jetties and boats into matchwood. The submersible reared up, clambering from the water, scraping its bulk over the edge of the harbour. The six legs straightened out and the *Neptune* towered twenty feet over the pirates who had resisted the urge to run. A moment of silence filled the square before the remaining buccaneers, as one, drew their pistols and carbines and opened fire at the invading contraption.

Bullets struck the *Neptune*'s carapace and ricocheted off in all directions, unable to penetrate the thick metal plating. The rebounding projectiles flew around the square, causing more damage to the pirates themselves than they did to the submersible. The *Neptune* strode forward over the cobbles, futile gunfire striking it from all sides. From his raised vantage point on the gallows, Jones watched as men attempted to rush beneath the mechanical creature, seeking some weaker point, only to be kicked aside or crushed by the *Neptune*'s heavy feet. He had to admit, the pirates were brave. Stupid, but brave.

In the first few moments as the *Neptune* rampaged ashore, the party on the platform stood motionless, mouths agape, transfixed by the unfolding carnage. Rackham was the first to recover, shoving Culpepper towards the stairs, shouting at Rook to get him to safety. The pirate captain moved to the edge of the platform, yelling instructions and gesturing to his men, who were by now too busy trying to avoid the metal beast in their midst to pay any attention to their leader.

The *Neptune* stomped around the square, sparks flying where its feet struck the cobbles. The deadly pincers swung this way and that, sending the quickest of the buccaneers diving for cover, and the slower, less lucky men, flying through the air.

A cannon roared and the *Neptune* staggered, struck in the side by the shot. Jones twisted to see a cloud of smoke roll up from the barrel of the weapon, manhandled round from its original position covering the bay. The submersible trembled and emitted an ear-splitting shriek as steam erupted from its damaged hull. The gun crew gave a ragged cheer as their metallic foe slumped to the ground, one of the leg mechanisms crumpling beneath it.

The *Neptune* lay like a wounded animal, limbs twitching, dented plates oozing a trail of thick black oil. The gun blasted out once again and the round smashed into the submersible's rear section – the armour plates buckling, great gouts of steam spewing out. The pirates around the square regrouped, closing in on the helpless craft, weapons raised.

At Rackham's instruction, one squad of men concentrated their fire on the observation dome. Here the bullets had more effect than against the riveted hull. Fractures spider-webbed across the glass under the barrage and Jones waited for the whole viewport to cave inward. But despite the cracks, despite the relentless hail of fire, somehow the dome held.

The submersible's frame jerked, the heavy feet scraping across the ground. Pistons straining amidst groans of protesting metal, the *Neptune* heaved upright, crabbing first one way and then the other as it compensated for the damaged leg. With a crunch of gears engaging, a pincer-tipped arm scythed down and across, toppling the squad of gunmen like ninepins, leaving them broken in the wake of its passage.

The cannon fired once more, but its crew had miscalculated, failing to account for their target's movement. The shot flew beneath the *Neptune*'s belly, bouncing headlong over the cobbles. The men around the gun scrabbled to reload as the submersible recovered its balance and rumbled into motion once more. It stomped into a turn, its cylindrical rear smashing through the corner of the tavern wall, scattering brick and timber.

The mechanical beast ripped its way through a pile of cargo, smashing crates and barrels aside. The massive claws opened with a sinister hiss and reached out, clamping around a wooden cart. With no more effort than a child might toss away an unwanted toy, the submersible flung the cart across the square. The improvised projectile flew true, crashing down on the gun emplacement, boards and axles cracking apart, separated wheels bouncing away over the stones. The cannon and the limp bodies of its crew lay broken and still beneath the wreckage.

With the pirates scattered and injured men littering the flagstones, the *Neptune* paused in its headlong rampage. It limped round in a full circle, seeking more adversaries. Finding none, the injured monster fixed its attention on the gallows where Rackham stood, transfixed by the carnage unleashed upon his men. As the submersible approached, the pirate shook free of his paralysis and made to flee. Turning from the chaos he came face-to-face with Jones, still teetering on tiptoe. Rackham leaned in close, eyes filled with rage.

"This won't stop me," he spat. "And it won't save you."

He reached for the trapdoor lever and pulled it. With a horrifying lurch, Jones dropped.

The fall was only inches, but it seemed to last forever before his descent was cruelly arrested by the noose. The drop wasn't so far as to break his neck, but the rude halt was more than enough to knock the breath from his lungs at the very moment the rope dug in, making the expelled air impossible to replace.

Dangling, bound hand and foot, Jones squirmed, the hemp at his throat a crushing iron trap. His chest heaved, the muscles in spasm as he tried to breathe. He was vaguely aware of the *Neptune*'s bulk as it lumbered closer, but his vision contracted into a narrow tunnel and his ears filled with the frantic pounding of his pulse. He spun at the end of the rope, limp, his existence reduced to a slow, grey dizziness.

The last shreds of his consciousness slipped away. The world swung first one way and then the other and then he was weightless, falling, floating, down into darkness.

*

Kowalski stood in the knee-high water, staring up at the tantalising circle of daylight, trying to work out what the hell was going on up above.

The noise of the blast had echoed down the shaft, bringing him to his feet. His ears caught the unmistakeable crack of gunfire, mingled with crashes and thumps, and the cries of men.

He hollered up the shaft. "Hey!"

A head appeared over the rim of the hole. The pirate who had hauled Jones away earlier scowled down at him. "What?"

"You having a little trouble up there?"

"Shut your trap," came the reply.

Another booming impact rang out, this one causing a noticeable tremor through the stones. The guard above sprang back, disappearing from Kowalski's narrow field of vision. A gunshot sounded, followed by a loud mechanical crunch and the smash of metal on stone.

Without warning the shaft was full of tumbling bricks and lengths of splintered timber. Kowalski crouched for cover, hands over his head. A hail of gravel and rock spattered down into the water, chunks of masonry sending up huge splashes. The roar of the descending wreckage filled the air, echoing around the narrow space. A lump of brickwork smashed into Kowalski's shoulder and he hunkered down under the avalanche of debris and noise, convinced he was about to be buried alive.

When the thunderous downfall subsided, he gingerly unfolded himself, sloughing off his crust of fragmented stone. A thick cloud of dust clogged the air, and Kowalski coughed, peering at the piles of rubble and jumble of timbers that surrounded him. It seemed someone had picked up an entire street's worth of houses and dropped them down the hole.

Looking up, he spotted a thick spar wedged across the width of the shaft directly above him. Lord bless that piece of wood, he thought. It had clearly acted as a shield, deflecting the largest lumps of tumbling stone.

And at least now he wasn't alone. There, inches above the water, sticking out from the chaos of bricks and broken beams, protruded a hand. Kowalski sloshed forward and tugged at the appendage. The arm flopped out from the debris, dislodging a tumble of gravel and revealing the face of his pirate guard, lifeless eyes staring out from the rubble.

Kowalski started to dig – crashes and hollow booms continuing to echo down from the conflict above.

*

The throb of the engine worked its way into Jones' awareness, a rhythmic match for the pounding ache in his temples. The particular tone of the machinery noise seemed familiar. He cracked open an eye and took in the curvature of the riveted plates above him. The *Neptune* – somehow he was inside the *Neptune*. And somehow he was still alive.

He crawled to the bulkhead and pulled himself into a seated position, groaning as he lifted his head, his vision swimming with the effort. Stabilising himself against the wall, he raised a hand to the tender skin of his throat, grimacing as he swallowed.

"*Senor* Jones, whatever is that terrible smell?"

Isabella peered down from the compartment's doorway. Jones gave a weak smile and indicated his filthy clothing.

"That would be me," he croaked. "I'm afraid my overnight lodgings were not quite the Mirador."

She moved closer, eyes travelling over his bruised and battered frame. She crouched down beside him and leant in, planting a kiss on his cheek.

"When I saw you on the gallows, I was sure we were too late," she said, dark eyes glistening.

"I'm a little stretched, but I'll survive. Here, help me up..."

With Isabella's assistance, Jones clambered to his feet. He swayed and his vision blurred once more, but he steadied himself and stared down at the woman. "What are you doing here?"

She batted her eyelashes and adopted a doe-eyed look. "I convinced your Lord Brunel to take me on an excursion. Somehow he found it impossible to refuse." She grinned, the girlish expression vanishing. "I think he is rather fond of me..."

Isabella remained at his side, supporting him as they made their way forward through the narrow companionway. The *Neptune* had been in the wars, that much was clear. Dirty water sloshed beneath the metal grilles of the companionways, sharp bursts of spray erupting from cracked bulkheads and misting the air. The crew scurried around, lugging spanners or repair plates, grim purpose etched in their faces.

The control room itself was awash, the deck inches deep. The great round dome was cracked and starred, trails of liquid seeping down its inside. Brunel turned from the watery gloom beyond the fractured glass and nodded to his passengers.

"Good to see you up old chap. I rather worried we had misjudged our timing."

"Tight timing or no, I appreciated the intervention." Jones gestured to the viewport. "Your vessel seems to have paid a high price for the effort."

The engineer grimaced. "I wouldn't trust us below twenty feet, but the pumps are coping for the moment."

"Good to hear. Now, forgive me, we have little time. How far to the *Great Eastern*? I have important information for London. We can't afford for Rackham to overtake us."

"All the stops are open, we're at full speed. Well, as fast as we can go in this state." The old man's frown gave way to a sly smile. "But I risked a deeper dive before our departure, improvising a little something to slow our friends down. Shame I used the demolition charge back at your execution, otherwise I could have put the bloody warship on the bottom of the bay."

Jones shook his head. "The dreadnought is the least of our concerns, if you can believe it. This affair has become more complicated than we thought. And much more serious to boot." He looked around the bridge. "I need to speak to Kowalski. Where is he?"

*

The streets around the square were in ruins, making Cayona look even more dilapidated, something Kowalski would have thought impossible. Buildings were missing walls and sections of roof, the displaced bricks and tiles scattered across the cobbled roads. Flames licked up amongst the damaged structures and everywhere there were wounded men. Some limped through the rubble, seeking their fellows, others sat with blood-soaked rags pressed to their wounds.

Kowalski overheard enough conversation to work out Brunel's submersible had made quite the nuisance of itself, tearing up buildings as it smashed its way through the streets. Wide-eyed accounts of the *Neptune*'s rampage were accompanied by dark glances cast towards the dreadnought out in the bay. It seemed her gunners' ill-advised attempts to drive off the mechanical monster had done nothing but add to the devastation. Poor Jack would have his hands full keeping the townsfolk happy after this little episode.

Liberating the padlock keys from the dead pirate had filled Kowalski with a burst of energy and enthusiasm, but hauling his leaden limbs up the ladder and out of the shaft had drained the reservoir. His legs and arms ached after his night of treading water and his face was scratched and bruised from the rubble shower he had endured.

Of Jones he could see no sign. He was sure this meant good news and the Englishman was still alive. He reckoned it would take a damned sight more than a gang of disorganised thugs to cause that one any real problems. Regardless of Jones' fate, Kowalski had to get out of Cayona. It would only be a matter of time before somebody realised their prisoner was missing.

The pirates of Tortuga had taken a bloody nose this morning – he sure didn't want to have them take out their frustration on him.

He pulled a piece of flapping curtain from the window of a wrecked house and wrapped a strip around his forehead, tugging it down over one eye, practically covering half his face. He fashioned a sling from the remaining material and tucked his arm inside. He was was banking on the fake bandages and his dishevelled appearance to ensure he fitted in with the other men moving about, but all the same he kept his head down as he hobbled through the streets.

He limped along the waterfront, heading for the docks at the edge of town. His night of captivity had been deeply unpleasant, and that kind of treatment always brought out the worst in him. Before he sought a way off Tortuga he was of a mind to see if he couldn't add to Calico Jack's woes.

*

Rackham watched as the squad of sailors gathered at the dreadnought's stern hauled in the line. The man clutching its end was hoisted up the ship's flank, spitting seawater onto the deck as he clambered over the side. He pulled the goggles from his face, bare chest heaving as he recovered from the dive. Rackham drummed his fingers on the rail, waiting for the report.

"There's a length of anchor chain fouling the screw," panted the diver. "Explains what the *Gertrude*'s doing over there..." He gestured towards the cliffs.

The crewmen turned as one. Across the bay a steamer rubbed against the rocks with the ebb and flow of the waves, wearing more holes into her patched and rusted hull.

"How long?" demanded Rackham.

The man shrugged. "I don't know. Yards of the bloody stuff I suppose."

Rackham's temper surged. He lashed out, swiping the diver with a vicious backhand. "Idiot," he snapped. "How long to get it cleared?"

The diver rubbed at his jaw, eyes downcast. "We'll have to cut it. Two hours? Maybe three?"

Rackham's fists tightened, his fingernails digging into his palms. He turned on the *Revenge*'s chief engineer. "I want this ship moving in an hour. Understood?"

The engineer hesitated. Time to make the consequences of failure clear, thought Rackham. "Mister Rook!" he called.

The Irishman materialised at his shoulder. "Aye sir?"

"Do everything you can to assist and ah, encourage, these gentlemen in their efforts to free the screw."

Rook tilted his plated head, a wicked grin creeping across his ravaged features. The crewmen shared nervous looks. "Why sir, it'll be my pleasure."

Evil little bastard, thought Rackham. He'll be hoping for a damned delay so he can enjoy making an example of someone. Rook's particular skills were often useful, but the man's predilection for cruelty could sometimes prove counterproductive. Best ensure this particular task was a genuine team effort.

"One hour Mister Rook," said Rackham. "Or it's your head too."

The ghastly smile faded. "Aye sir," muttered the Irishman.

Rackham turned away from the stern and made his way forward. He flexed his knuckles, hand still tingling where it had struck the hapless diver. The sudden release of violence had felt good. More of that might be in order if things didn't start going his way.

*

Kowalski approached the warehouse only to have his path blocked by the burly seaman who stood watch at its doors. The sailor regarded him from beneath a heavy brow, taking in the filthy clothes and bandages.

"What do you want?" he grunted.

Kowalski jerked a thumb towards the town. "Jack wants every able-bodied man in the square. He's mustering a crew to take off after that steel lobster."

The brute pondered this, then swung his head from side to side. "Got to stay here. Jack said so."

"And now he says otherwise. I'm taking your place." Kowalski indicated his bandaged arm. "I ain't no use to them with this..."

The sailor rubbed his unshaven chin with tattooed knuckles. "S'pose not," he said eventually. The guard pulled a pistol from his belt and Kowalski's stomach lurched, but the weapon was turned and offered grip-first to him.

"Here. You've to put a bullet in any feller who tries to talk his way past."

"Will do," nodded Kowalski gravely.

The sailor padded off towards the town.

Thank the Lord for the less-than-bright, thought Kowalski. How would the rest of us get by without them? He slipped through the narrow gap in the doors and into the warehouse.

He pulled the fake bandages off and threw them aside as he made his way between the stacks of crates. The illicit cargo was still where it had been placed the previous evening, piled up in the clear space at the warehouse's centre. Kowalski eyed the fat hessian sacks with distaste. Some of his fellow mercenaries swore by the stuff – the airmen in particular. But he'd never seen the attraction. Black coffee and strong tobacco worked fine for him, he'd never felt the need to resort to the Bolivian Marching Powder.

Atop a barrel alongside the sacks was the equipment tipped from his and Jones' packs the night before. Kowalski rummaged through the climbing gear and rations before his hand closed around the hard metallic sphere of one of Ramon Cuervo's explosive charges. Perfect.

With the sharp point of a climbing piton he sawed at the sackcloth of one of the lower bags. When the hole was big enough, he turned the dial on the clockwork timer and set the orb quietly ticking, then shoving the charge into the bag, pushing it as far as he could into the chalky beige paste. Regardless of what else happened, this particular batch of Bolivia's finest wouldn't be making Culpepper a single cent.

Kowalski stepped out of the gloom of the warehouse, emerging blinking into the light. The sun bounced from the waters of the bay, forcing him to squint as he ran his eyes over the boats moored along the harbour. Whilst the warehouse guard clearly hadn't been the sharpest tool in the box, even he'd eventually work out he'd been duped. Kowalski reckoned he didn't have long before the brute would come lumbering back along the waterfront, buddies in tow. He wanted to be well on his way by then.

His eye fixed on the sleek lines of Culpepper's launch, tied to the wharf a short distance from the warehouse. Her two crewmen stood idly, smoking cigarettes and leaning on the stern rail. Kowalski tucked the pistol away into the back of his belt and made his way down the wooden jetty towards the launch. He figured if he was going to borrow a boat, he might as well leave town in style.

The flat crump of an explosion rolled out from the building behind him and the sailors' heads whipped round seeking the source of the noise. Their eyes flitted between the man on the jetty and the trails of smoke curling out of the warehouse door. Neither man seemed overly alarmed, likely inured to such blasts following the excitement of the morning's events. The sailors appeared unarmed too, which was a relief. Made it less likely there would be any foolish heroics.

Kowalski pasted a broad smile onto his face.

"How you doing boys? Any chance of a smoke?"

*

Rackham made his way up the ladders towards the *Revenge*'s bridge, anger pounding behind his eyes with every step. He had rushed out to his ship, determined to pursue the mechanical menace out to sea, only to be baulked when the dreadnought refused to move. The enforced delay added to the rage bubbling in his veins, but denied the release of action and pursuit, he was forced to think. Even if the *Revenge* was temporarily incapacitated, he refused to sit idly by whilst his tormentors got clean away. He kicked open the bridge door and snapped instructions to the sailor sitting before the wireless.

"Get the airship aloft. That thing that attacked us must have come from a ship. A nearby one. I want it found."

The crewman lifted the flared trumpet of the mouthpiece and began to relay the orders to shore.

Rackham stood, fists clenched, surveying his fleet. It rankled sending a damned balloon out, but needs must. On principle, he harboured a deep resentment towards flying machines and their pilots, holding them responsible for the gradual shifting of trade from the ocean into the air. He could smell the end of piracy in the change. But for the moment, the clumsy dirigible offered a better chance of finding his enemy than all the vessels at his disposal.

All those ships. All those guns. More firepower than even Teach or Morgan could have dreamed of, and yet that bloody machine had waltzed in and out of the bay with barely a scratch. The only shots the *Revenge* had fired had missed the submersible completely, doing nothing but more damage to his town.

The whole thing had been a shambles. Made him look like a fool, unable to hang onto a couple of prisoners. There would be questions amongst the Brethren – whispered at first, but they'd grow louder if the attackers weren't caught, and quickly. Frustration banged around inside his skull once again.

"Not your finest hour Mister Rackham," said Culpepper's voice behind him. "Your incompetence has risked exposing our activities."

Rackham whirled on the American, pushing close, his face inches from the other man's. "Don't try to blame this on me," he snarled. Culpepper's podgy countenance darkened, but Rackham ploughed on, unwilling to let the pompous American speak. "You told me he was a journalist," he roared. "You think a bloody writer has access to machinery like that?" The Commodore reared back from the tirade and Rackham pressed forward, pointed finger raised in the other man's face. "And you,

you damned fool. Couldn't keep your fat mouth shut. Had to go blabbing off about your ridiculous scheme."

The American's nostrils flared and he found his voice. "The only thing ridiculous here is you and your ragtag bunch of cut-throats."

Cut-throats is it? Rackham's mind filled with the image of Culpepper's blood spewing from a ragged slit in his fleshy neck, down over the ever-so-smart uniform. God but that would be a satisfying sight.

A costly one though – the Commodore was still worth more to him alive than he was dead, despite any short-term satisfaction gutting him might provide. Rackham hauled his temper into check, packing it away for future use. He fixed the American with a flinty gaze.

"And yet this ragtag bunch are all that stands between you and a noose. Assuming, that is, you want us to go and catch the bastards for you, rather than doing it for yourself?"

Culpepper stared at him, face flushed with anger but unable to deny the point. "Distasteful as it may be," he said eventually, "it appears I still have need of your services."

Damn right you do, you arrogant arsehole, thought Rackham.

The American turned away from their exchange and waved a sailor over, his casual command of the pirate crew, without so much as a by-your-leave, causing Rackham's blood to pound once more.

"Call my launch. Have them come alongside." Culpepper returned his attention to Rackham. "I shall depart for Havana. Inform me when the situation is resolved." The eyes in the fat face narrowed. "Don't let me down."

Rackham stared out at the wreckage of his town, the broken buildings and curls of smoke stinging at his pride.

"I'm not doing it for you," he said.

*

Windward Passage

The excursion pool became a cauldron of churning water as the dark shape of the *Neptune* rose through the gap in the hull. The submersible blew the last of her ballast and broke the surface, water streaming from her riveted plating. Turner looked down from the gantry, taking in the bent metalwork and the starburst cracks across the glass dome. Brunel's pride and joy appeared to have taken something of a beating.

The submersible's upper hatch cracked open and Jones' head emerged.

"Thank God you're back," Turner called. "We feared the worst."

The army man gave him a tired nod in return, reaching down to offer a hand to the De La Vega woman. Turner frowned, reminded of the argument before the *Neptune's* departure. Dead-set against letting a female passenger aboard the submersible, Turner had been unable to reason with Brunel. The woman from Havana appeared to have the old man twisted around her little finger.

With a hiss of hydraulic pressure the engineer himself rose from the craft's innards.

"The worst very nearly occurred," said Brunel. "The Major here was late for his rendezvous. We found him just in time."

"Where is Captain Kowalski?" asked Turner, becoming aware of the downcast faces opposite.

Jones raised weary eyes. "He won't be joining us. We left him behind." The voice was dejected, edged with bitterness.

Brunel stared up from his chair. "Not through choice, Major. How many more times do I need to repeat myself? We practically tore the town apart looking for him."

Jones straightened his shoulders, mastering himself. When he spoke once more, his voice held a note of contrition.

"My apologies. You couldn't have done any more. Not once Rackham began to bombard his own town."

Mollified, Brunel nodded and reached for the control stick on his wheelchair. Turner watched the engineer lead the party over the gangplank, amazed as ever at the old man's stamina. Despite the extended stay at the controls of the submersible, the engineer appeared his usual spritely, cantankerous, brilliant self. He seemed in considerably better shape, in fact, than the man trailing behind. Jones looked exhausted, and from the sounds of it, had enjoyed the dubious hospitality of the Tortugan pirates. Turner itched to hear the tale, but more pressing matters awaited.

"Excuse me. I must return to the bridge and get a message to the *Iris*. Commander Warburton has been insisting we head to a friendly harbour and report you as missing."

Brunel's mechanised chair headed for the pressure hatch. "I believe we could all do with some fresh air. Much as I love the old *Neptune*, it is rather like being packed inside a tin can."

They trooped through the engine room to the ship's elevator. Turner slid the doors closed and pushed the selector lever to the topmost position. The conveyance gave a shudder and started upward.

"Warburton will be relieved," said Turner. "He's become rather frustrated – both with the lack of news, and our inability to discuss matters properly."

Brunel looked up, a quizzical frown in place.

"It's been like the old days," explained Turner. "We're reduced to sending messages by shutter lantern. Bloody wireless is playing up. Can't get through to anyone."

*

With a jerk the elevator came to a halt and the doors slid open, the passengers emerging into the wheelhouse. Sunlight flooded in, sparkling off the gentle waves. Bloody weather, thought Jones. Better a storm. Or fog, or mist – anything to help them slip away. On a glorious afternoon like this, the bulk of the *Great Eastern* would be visible for miles.

The deck officer stepped forward and snapped off a salute. "Welcome back Your Lordship."

"Thank you Mister Jenson," answered Brunel. "Now get on the lantern and tell our Navy chums we're back –"

"And tell them we need to get moving. Now." All heads turned in Jones' direction.

"There's nothing wrong with your wireless," he said. "This is Rackham's doing." He went on, ignoring Turner's incredulous look. "There's a dreadnought on its way Captain. We need to get out of here as fast as we bloody well can –"

The conversation came to an abrupt halt as the unmistakeable sound of an explosion rattled the bridge windows. Heads snapped round to see a huge plume of spray raining back down onto the sea's surface a hundred yards in front of their Royal Navy escort.

"What on earth?" blurted Jenson.

"Range-finding shot," said Jones. They had already run out of time.

As he spoke, another fountain of water erupted, closer to the *Iris* this time, followed a moment later by the noise of the blast. Jones winced. Their escort's guns couldn't match the range of those on Rackham's warship. When the pirate gunners got their eye in, the cruiser would be pounded into the sea before she could return a single shot.

"There's your dreadnought..." said Turner, pointing south and handing over a spyglass. "By the size of her bow wave, she's making at least twenty knots."

"Faster than us I presume?" asked Jones, raising the telescope.

"We'll do fourteen. Maybe fifteen at a pinch. With our paddles we're much more manoeuvrable, despite the difference in size, but a screw-driven warship will have this old girl for speed every time."

Jones watched through the lens as a bright muzzle flash erupted from the dreadnought. Long seconds later the shell struck home, the shot finding its mark this time. A cloud of black smoke burst up from the cruiser and, moments later, the mournful sound of an alarm klaxon echoed across the stretch of water between the ships.

All activity on the bridge came to a halt, the crewmen frozen, appalled at the scene. The men of the *Great Eastern* had clearly spent their war years very far from the bloodstained waters of the North Sea. A second impact rocked the *Iris*, and a third. More smoke darkened the air, and the orange glint of flames could be seen.

It was Isabella who broke the silence. "We must do something..."

The woman's voice seemed to break the spell transfixing Turner. He tore himself away from the window and bellowed into a tube, his voice echoing out from speakers throughout the vessel. "All hands! All hands! Launch the starboard boats."

As the crew burst into activity, preparing to mount their rescue effort, Jones regarded the stricken ship across the water. She had already adopted a noticeable list, her deck leaning away from them, the rust-streaked plating of her lower hull lifting into view.

"Captain, our time is short..."

Turner spun to face him, face like thunder. "If you're suggesting we abandon those sailors, you're not the man I thought you were Major."

"You misunderstand. I would never suggest such a thing. But we need to think about our own vessel."

Brunel bristled. "This ship can take a lot more punishment than our unfortunate escort."

"I don't believe sinking us is in Rackham's plan. He hasn't taken a potshot at us yet which rather suggests he's seeking a new addition for his fleet. Rackham is a showman – he won't be able to resist a temptation like the *Great Eastern*."

"This ship?" spluttered Brunel. "In the hands of pirates? Over my dead body."

Jones stared down at the old man in the wheelchair. "Your Lordship, I fear that's exactly what Calico Jack has in mind."

"What do you suggest?"

Jones regarded the speck on the southern horizon and then turned his attention to the more immediate scene as the *Great Eastern*'s boats headed for the stricken cruiser. The *Iris* was now keeled over almost ninety degrees, the remaining crew leaping into the water and swimming for the approaching lifeboats. It would be a matter of minutes before the water found the hungry openings of her twin funnels. From there it would be sucked down into her belly, condemning her to the deep.

"We can't outrun the dreadnought, but we might at least draw her away from the boats." He gestured to the rescue flotilla. "We'll never get them back aboard in time, and I dread to think what Rackham will do to them. I doubt he's in the mood to take on passengers."

Turner contemplated the view outside the window and nodded. "Go on..." he said.

"If it's the *Great Eastern* Rackham wants, let's at least make him work for it."

Brunel moved the control stick on his wheelchair, turning away from the windows. "I'd sooner see this vessel on the bottom than part of a pirate fleet."

"If the situation requires it, I shall see it done," said Turner, steel in his voice.

Jones regarded the sailor. "No you won't Captain. I commandeered your vessel. No need for you to go down with it." He held up a hand to silence Turner's protestations. "I'll be leading Rackham on this merry chase. Get your crew into the remaining boats." Turner's frown deepened but Jones continued. "I admire your sense of duty. But the Admiralty placed you at my disposal, and I've just given you an order."

Brunel's chair trundled forward between the two men. The engineer stared up at the *Great Eastern*'s master. "By playing the Admiralty card, I do believe the Major is holding trumps. It's time to look to your crew's safety. The ship belongs to Major Jones now."

Turner's shoulders slumped and he gave a reluctant nod. "Very well," he said. "Mister Jenson, signal the men to abandon ship. All hands to the boats."

Emergency klaxons began to sound throughout the vessel, and the crewmen in the wheelhouse made for the companionway. Turner and Brunel conferred briefly before the old man spoke to Isabella.

"My dear, I would be happier if you would accompany myself and Captain Turner in the *Neptune*. It may be bashed and bruised, but it will still provide a more comfortable ride than an open rowboat."

Isabella ignored Brunel, stepping close to Jones, scowling up at him. "For this you throw your life away? You men are all the same. Always looking for a cause worth dying for..."

Once again Jones found himself at a loss for words to respond to this woman. Looking down into Isabella's black gaze he knew he could never make her understand. He made do with a shrug.

The gesture infuriated the Cuban woman. She swung her hand, catching Jones across the cheek with a sharp slap that echoed around the wheelhouse. His face stung from the contact and he couldn't help but flinch as the arm was raised again. However, this time Isabella's hand anchored around his neck and pulled his face down to hers, her lips locking onto his own.

Before he realised what was happening the woman broke away, heading for the door. At the threshold she turned, dark eyes blazing.

"Perhaps *senor*, there are some causes worth living for, no?" With that, she left.

Jones felt the colour rise in his face. The flush of embarrassment would at least mask the tingling redness from where she had slapped him. Speechless he looked to the remaining occupants of the wheelhouse. Turner stood open-mouthed in astonishment, whilst Brunel chuckled at Jones' discomfort.

"I suggest you make it out of this adventure alive Major," said the old man. "Because Miss De La Vega will surely kill you if you don't."

*

"Gunners say she's in range Cap'n," shouted the young sailor standing by the rank of speaking tubes.

Rackham turned from the window. "She's been in range for some time now Billy. Please inform the gunners that when I require their advice, I will ask for it."

The sailor blanched at Rackham's tone, flicking the cover up from a tube and muttering into the opening. Rackham shook his head and turned to Rook.

"All those idiots want to do is fire their bloody guns."

The Irishman looked up from his chair. "Shouldn't give them such big toys to play with. What do you expect?"

"I expect them to do as they're told."

Rook scratched at the plating on his head, picking flakes of rust from the metal and dropping them onto the deck. "The boys don't understand what you want with that ship. Can't say I blame them overmuch. Not rightly sure I understands it myself."

Rackham bent down and spoke into the man's ear, his voice low and hard.

"You don't need to understand Rooky-boy. You're just like the others. All you need to do is what you're told." He placed a hand on the Irishman's shoulder, stopping him from rising. "Easy now. No need to get uppity. Always remember, these men won't follow you. They hate you a lot more than they hate me."

And I've been very careful to keep it that way, thought Rackham as Rook glowered up at him. Using the Irishman as an instrument of discipline meant the Brethren universally loathed his lieutenant. Much more so than the Captain who ordered the punishments in the first place. A strong second-in-command was necessary – but no point letting them get too popular, or developing ideas above their station.

"You're a good lad. With a talent for dirty work. But don't ever be thinking it makes you Captain material."

Rook stared up at him, the living portion of his face twisted in sullen anger. After a moment, the Irishman muttered an "Aye sir," and looked away, acknowledging his place in the proper order of things.

"Good boy," said Rackham. He rapped his fist on the man's iron skull. "Now make yourself useful. Go and kill some Englishmen for me..."

Whoever remained on the *Great Eastern* must have thought Rackham was stupid – banking on him being so intent on his prey he would ignore the lifeboats she had left in her wake. They would enjoy no such luck, nor receive any mercy.

Rackham made his way out onto the wing of the bridge. Down on the main deck his sailors were untying the ropes securing the squat shape of the gunboat. Shallow of draught and mighty fast, the gunboat had proven herself on many a smuggling expedition. Now she was hoisted aloft by lines at her stern and bow, the derricks swinging round, taking her out over the side rail. The crew clambered aboard and the winch turned, lowering her until the keel hung scant feet from the waters thundering down the dreadnought's flank.

Rook arrived on the deck below. He clambered up onto the rail, balancing there for a moment before launching himself outwards. He flew out and down, arresting his fall on the rope supporting the gunboat's stern. Hanging there, the Irishman looked up to the bridge, sunlight glistening off his metallic plating. He waved a hand in a salute and Rackham nodded in return.

Rook wrapped a leg around the line and slid down in a controlled descent, hopping away from the rope onto the deck beside the helmsman.

With Rackham's lieutenant aboard, the cables were released and the gunboat splashed down into the waves. The prow dug in to the surging spray and for a moment she seemed sure to founder, but her screw bit at the water and she levelled her trim. The small vessel turned away to port and steamed hard towards the lifeboats clustered around the upturned hull of the cruiser. Rackham eyed the defenceless flotilla in the distance – another load of English sailors to feed the sharks.

He returned his attention to the *Great Eastern*. Bursts of spray shot up on either side of the hull where the ship's massive paddles thrashed at the water. By God but they were driving her hard. Whoever stood at the helm of the enormous merchant ship was pushing her to her limits. And all for nothing. Her flight was futile – the *Revenge* visibly closing the gap with every passing moment.

The thrill of the chase gripped him again, his blood pounding as it had when the airship's captain had first radioed him with news of the ship lying offshore. He gripped the rail and gave a fierce smile. Not long now, and she would be his – the prize jewel in England's maritime crown, very nearly in his grasp.

*

Alarm bells clamoured for attention and warning lamps winked urgently above the gauges, every indicator needle quivering in the red. Jones could not have said what information the dials were designed to impart in the first place, so he did the only thing he could and ignored them all.

The telegraph levers for each paddle wheel were pushed forward to the stops and the *Great Eastern* thundered across the water, requiring a tight grasp on the helm to keep her heading fixed. Exactly what her heading was remained a mystery, the compass needle spinning crazily in its housing, useless within the magnetic disturbance created by Rackham's ship. All Jones was sure of was that every passing second drew them further away from the helpless lifeboats and the *Iris*.

The deck shook beneath Jones' feet as the engines pounded away – boiler pressures and paddle speeds no doubt far in excess of what Brunel had envisaged. Thus far the vessel was holding together, despite the shaking, a testament to the engineer's skill.

Jones looked aft through the rear windows. There, barely a quarter mile behind, closing on the starboard quarter, was the sinister shape of the dreadnought, black clouds belching up from her trio of smokestacks. The warship cut through the water, her fearsome speed putting the lie to her decrepit appearance as she closed in on her quarry.

Time was running out. The dreadnought would catch the *Great Eastern* in minutes. He could do no more. The ship was lost – what remained was to decide the manner of the grand vessel's passing.

*

Jenson stood in the stern of the lifeboat, supervising as the last of the survivors was hauled spluttering from the water.

The white hulls of the open boats were floating low, laden with men rescued from the cruiser. The *Iris* herself had slipped beneath the surface moments before, a patch of oily water dotted with bobbing debris the only remaining evidence of her existence.

The sound of an engine brought his head up and he spotted a squat vessel closing on the pack of milling lifeboats. The new arrival coasted to a halt, bobbing in the swell fifty yards away from the nearest craft. A figure stood in her bows behind a formidable-looking machine gun, his misshapen face cracking into an awful smile as he reached for the crank handle.

Bullets flew from the revolving muzzle in a terrible mechanised fusillade. Jenson stood transfixed as fountains of water sprang up, marching over the surface, the procession of splashes dragging his gaze along with its progress. The hail of lead reached one of the boats, the impacts tossing chunks of wood and men into the air. The helpless crewmen packed into the lifeboat jerked in a gruesome dance, tugged this way and that as the bullets flew in. Only a handful of the sailors survived this first barrage, leaping into the water on the opposite side from their assailant – the possibility of drowning or sharks proving less immediate than the threat of the gunman.

The harsh chatter of the gun fell silent and cries and moans from the men on the decimated boat drifted over the water, carried on a breeze stinking of cordite and blood. It took Jenson a moment to comprehend the next sound he registered, so alien was it to the scene. Shrill laughter rang out from the man in the gunboat's bow.

Recovering from their shock, the sailors in the lifeboats scrabbled for their oars, desperate to put distance between themselves and the madman on the gunboat. But the flotilla was packed too tight and the oars only clattered against one another or made ineffective swipes at the water.

Jenson's boat had moved no more than half a dozen yards before the fearsome machine gun was hauled round in their direction.

*

The *Revenge* ploughed through the water, her course parallel with the larger vessel. They had caught up with the *Great Eastern* easily and now Rackham chafed, irritated by the stubbornness exhibited in his quarry's continued flight.

"Billy," he called. "Tell the boys to shove a couple of rounds past her wheelhouse. Past it mind – not through it. I'll have their hides if they so much as scratch her."

The sailor relayed the instructions through the speaking tube and Rackham stepped out of the wheelhouse. He looked down to the main deck, watching the heavy turrets grind round, the long guns rising to the required elevation.

The muzzle flashes were brighter than the sun, leaving after images behind his eyelids when he blinked. His ears rang as the wave of noise rolled out, rattling the windows behind him. The shells moved too fast for the eye to follow, but the shriek as they tore through the air gave an indication of their course.

A second after the guns sounded, two mountainous splashes erupted in the water beyond the merchant ship. The crew lined up along the dreadnought's rail gave a ragged cheer.

The huge vessel steamed on, paddles working as hard as ever. Rackham's irritation bubbled up into naked anger, becoming a physical thing trapped inside his head, seeking release. Seems they'd have to put some scratches in his quarry after all – maybe some holes too.

He waved down to the sailors manning the variety of weapons mounted on the port rails.

"Right lads," he yelled over the wind. "I've had enough. Put in the windows on her bridge. Everything but the big guns."

The men turned to their weapons, eager to have their fun. Fuses were lit, crank handles turned, and triggers were pulled along the length of the ship's rail. Rackham thrilled to the sound of a hundred carbines and swivel cannon unleashing hell against the enormous craft that had the temerity to defy his will.

*

The distant rumble of gunfire startled Jenson, breaking his rapt fascination with the gaping muzzle pointing his way.

"Get over the side!" he shouted, pushing the nearest men towards the side. A futile gesture, but he was damned if he'd simply stand there and let them all be shot. He looked back across the water, a sick knot forming in his stomach as the gunner fixed him with his uneven stare.

Suddenly, the sea beneath the gunboat boiled upwards, and she lurched, tipping over at a sharp angle, pirates tumbling over the rails and into the turbulent waters below. Amidst fountains of spray, the *Neptune* surged to the surface, smashing the gunboat aside, staving in its keel.

The submersible reared over the floundering vessel, mechanical arms raised, pincer claws spread wide. The arms hung there for an awful moment before plummeting down, flattening the wheelhouse and knocking the remaining crew from the buckled deck – all bar the figure who managed to stay balanced in the bow, hanging on to the gun mounting.

As the boat pitched and tossed from the impact, the pirate hauled his weapon round towards the submersible. The barrels spun, the gun's bark accompanied by high-pitched ricochets as bullets bounced from the *Neptune*'s plating. A metal limb swept up from the water once more, pistons extending as it snapped out with terrible speed, grasping both man and machine gun in the steel grip of the claw.

Clamped around the chest, mashed together with the wreckage of the gun, the pirate howled as he was lifted into the air, his unnatural features stretched into a hideous scream. Higher and higher rose the arm, accompanied by the rising pitch of the trapped man's screeching. Finally, at the apex of the submersible's reach, fifteen feet above the water, the blades of the claw snicked horribly together and separated sections of man and machinery tumbled into the sea.

Stumbling to the lifeboat's stern, flooded with a mixture of horror and relief, Jenson dropped to his knees and threw up over the side.

*

The roar of the small arms broadside from the dreadnought carried to Jones even over the thunderous vibration caused by the *Great Eastern*'s exertions. A handful of scattered impacts cracked the panes of the starboard windows and then, in an avalanche of noise and glass and splinters, the gunners on the ship opposite found their mark.

Jones threw himself to the deck, scrabbling into the shelter of a control console as the windows exploded inward, showering him with fragments of glass. He hunkered down out of the storm, the air filled with the angry buzz of bullets, as if a swarm of wasps had been released into the wheelhouse.

Rounds smacked into the banks of dials, shattering the glass of the gauges and clipping pipework. Sharp squeals of steam added to the bedlam, jets of billowing vapour clouding the air. Jones smelled smoke and grimaced as the hungry orange flicker of flames bloomed to the rear of the compartment where a spark must have found the stacks of charts.

Something a hell of a lot bigger than a bullet blasted through the wooden panelling inches from his head, shrapnel whistling past, a hot streak of pain lancing down his cheek. He touched trembling fingers to his face, the tips coming away crimson. Too close, too bloody close by half.

The incoming barrage seemed to fall away in intensity, or perhaps Jones had simply got used to it. Either way, he had to see what was going on. He crawled across the deck, trying to avoid the worst shards of metal and glass with limited success.

He raised himself to his knees by the helm, making the most of the insubstantial cover offered by the brass column and the wheel. His raised line of sight revealed the view through the shattered windows in the starboard bulkhead.

The dreadnought was closing the gap, the stretch of water between the two vessels down to a hundred yards. Keeping as low as he could, he lifted Turner's eyeglass and pulled it open, raising it to bring the pirate ship into sharp focus.

Rackham's vessel swarmed with sailors, although most appeared to have abandoned their guns, explaining the reduced amount of lead flying in his direction. Instead the men opposite were now engaged in preparing coils of rope, vicious-looking hooks dangling from the lines.

They were getting ready to board the *Great Eastern*, that much was clear. The dreadnought would pull alongside, matching speed with the merchant ship, and the grappling hooks would fly. Of course, Jones could veer away, putting off the inevitable, perhaps even sending some pirates tumbling into the waves, but Rackham had men to spare, and wouldn't give a fig how many of them died. He'd bring the dreadnought in again, keeping at it until the boarders finally made it up the sheer sides of the hull. Or more likely, he'd lose all patience and settle for putting a couple of rounds from his long guns into the wheelhouse, ending the chase for good.

Jones snapped the telescope shut and ran his gaze around the ruined bridge as isolated bursts of gunfire continued to whistle overhead. The bulkhead walls were riddled with holes, the glass panes from the windows now redistributed in razor fragments over every surface. Steam jetted from a hundred burst pipes, mixing with the acrid smoke billowing up from the fire amongst the charts. The flames had taken proper hold now, licking up the wooden panelling of the rear wall.

Who was he kidding? The chase was at an end already. He hauled himself to his feet, ignoring the ricochets. He stared across at the dreadnought, a thin smile forming on his lips.

"Plenty of guns on that ship of yours Jack," he said to himself, gripping the helm with one hand and reaching out for the telegraph levers with the other. "But how's her turning circle?"

Bracing himself, he spun the wheel to the right and threw the starboard paddle control to 'Full Astern'.

*

A brutal crunch of machinery rang out from the innards of the *Great Eastern*, the mechanical clamour echoing across the water, causing the pirate crew to turn as one from their boarding preparations.

The vast ship groaned and visibly shuddered, her deck pitching to starboard as the near side paddle abruptly changed direction.

Water blasted upward where the wheel gouged at the sea. From his elevated position on the bridge, Rackham saw first one, then another of the blades wrench free from their mountings and skip away across the surface before disappearing beneath the waves.

The great ship pitched further, heeled over hard as the paddle bit in. Machinery and material slid down her inclined planking, smashing into the starboard rail, barrels and crates bouncing up and over the obstacle, tumbling into the water.

Howling in metallic protest, the seven hundred feet of the *Great Eastern* surged round – impossibly fast, impossibly huge. Rackham stood open-mouthed, frozen in place as the bows of the merchant ship swung into the path of the dreadnought.

Awful comprehension of the sudden danger blossomed in his mind and he threw himself at the wheelhouse door, bursting inward and screaming at the transfixed helmsman.

"Hard-a-starboard!"

The sailor snapped from his trance, spinning the wheel, trying to turn the *Revenge* away from the looming hull of the *Great Eastern*, now perpendicular across their course and only fifty yards ahead.

The dreadnought's bow began to move, but too slowly, too late. She thundered onward, straight for the riveted plates of the vessel blocking their way.

Rackham gripped the rail beneath the windows, staring forward, unable to look away. A helpless rage burned within him as the gap between the ships disappeared.

*

The force of the impact threw Jones from the helm and across the wheelhouse. He smacked down hard on the deck, sliding sideways before coming to an abrupt and painful halt against the bulkhead. Something cracked in his side and he released a roar of agony.

In tears of pain he rolled over and gingerly pressed a hand to his torso. At least one rib, he thought, sucking in sharp shallow breaths through gritted teeth. Bloody sore, but it won't kill you. Stop whining. Worry about it later.

He pulled himself up, shuffling forward to see how much of a mess he'd made. The carnage that presented itself was well worth a broken bone or two – he had never seen anything like it.

A quarter of the way down the *Great Eastern*'s starboard side, beyond the still-churning paddle, the ship was rent by a massive fracture – the plates of the hull buckled and torn, the planking of the deck splintered upwards and out. From up on the bridge, Jones could see down into the gaping wound. There, plunged into the heart of the great vessel like an axe head, was the foremost twenty feet of the dreadnought.

Although rusted and patched, the warship's armour plating had sliced through the thinner hull of the merchant vessel like a hot knife through butter. Now the two ships ground against one another, the dreadnought's screw continuing to flail at the water, driving her deeper into the side of her quarry, whilst the *Great Eastern*'s thrashing paddles impaled her sideways on the sharp prow.

The tall smokestack nearest the impact point leaned drunkenly and then toppled forward, adding to the cacophony of screeching metalwork. The entire vessel shuddered beneath Jones' feet and the fracture cracked wider, another section of planking splintering up as the dreadnought lurched forward, penetrating further.

Jones became aware of the figure on the warship's bridge, waving his arms at a crew only just picking themselves up from where the collision had tossed them. Rackham – trying to regain control.

Jones smiled through the pain from his ribs. Not quite what you'd had planned, eh Jack?

Someone on the dreadnought finally thought to throw her engines into reverse, attempting to withdraw her bow from where it cleaved into the merchant vessel. The noise of tortured metal from the fracture grew in intensity as the warship tried to pull free, but the tangle of steel held fast.

Jones reached for a lever on the panel before him – the only control beyond steering and throttle he had asked Turner to explain. He threw the lever and felt a low tremor rumble its way up from below. Deep in the bowels of the ship, vents had just opened, releasing the air in the pressurised compartments, allowing the ocean to flood in through the excursion pool. The *Great Eastern* was going to the bottom, and she would be taking Rackham's pride and joy with her.

The fire in the wheelhouse crackled up, smoke finally overcoming steam in the two-way contest to fill the compartment. Struggling to breathe, Jones lurched out onto the wing of the bridge, injured ribs complaining as he coughed the vapours from his lungs. He wheezed his way down the ladder towards the main deck, clutching the rail with one hand and his aching side with the other.

He turned toward the stern and the welcome sight of the last of the ship's lifeboats. He limped aft, up the noticeable incline of the planks, reaching the lifeboat's davits and grasping hold of the rungs of the rope ladder. Before taking on the climb, he paused to look back along the side of the ship.

The *Great Eastern* had taken on a sharp slant, down at the bow as water poured into her interior. This in turn had dragged the front section of the dreadnought downwards, hoisting the screw at her stern clear of the water. The brass blades of the warship's propeller now churned air rather than the ocean, powerless to drag the trapped vessel free.

Jones watched as the dreadnought's crew began lowering boats over the side, abandoning any attempts to save their ship, concentrating instead on saving their own skins. The figure on the bridge opposite gesticulated at his men. The King of the Pirates seemed less than impressed with the misfortune dealt his beloved vessel. The man's helpless rage confirmed it for Jones – without the warship, Rackham was nothing. The task handed him in France was complete.

He contemplated the waiting lifeboat then turned his gaze back to Rackham, black emotion clouding out thoughts of escape. The job might be done, but his brother was still dead. And that bastard over there was still alive.

Jones turned away from the boat and staggered forward, heading for where the two ships ground against one another, locked together in a deadly embrace.

*

Billy shouted across the wheelhouse, the words lost amidst the noise of the dreadnought's suffering. Rackham lifted his head.

"What?"

"It's time to go Cap'n." The sailor gestured towards the door. "We've stripped all the guns we can, but we've run out of time. She's going down."

Rackham's temper surged up inside him. He hurled the glass from his hand. The improvised missile flew across the compartment, smashing against the bulkhead by Billy's head.

"You think I need you to tell me she's sinking?" he roared. "Get out of here. Wait for me at the boat."

Rackham raised the rum bottle and swigged from it, sucking air over his teeth as the raw spirit burned its way down his throat. Billy continued to hover in the doorway, shifting from one foot to the other, casting nervous glances through the forward windows. Rackham hauled his pistol from his belt and waved it at the sailor.

"Get going," he snarled. "Before I put a bullet through you..."

Billy turned and fled from his Captain's wrath. Rackham gave a snort of disgust and tossed the pistol over his shoulder. He pulled himself up from the chair, stumbling as he compensated for the angle of the deck. He stared out through the windows, down the length of the dreadnought to her bow, now scant feet above the roiling water.

The forward portion of the *Great Eastern* too was nearly submerged, the two vessels drowning together, dragging each other in, sucking all his plans down with them. The debacle at the hanging had been bad enough, but losing the *Revenge* would surely spell the end. The Brethren would never follow a Captain who had lost the biggest ship to ever fly the colours. Quietly, behind his back, there would be a ballot. The newly-elected Captain would put a round between Jack's eyes, or cut his throat, and that would be that.

Such dreams he'd had, such schemes. All for naught. He lifted the bottle again, spilling rum down his chin as the ship lurched, forcing him to grab at the rail to keep his footing. The waves lapped at the deck, the dreadnought slipping further into the sea, her armour plates twisting, rivets popping like firecrackers. Looking away from his tortured ship, he scowled towards the *Great Eastern*'s superstructure, where flames poured up from the bridge windows. He raised the bottle in a toast. Hope you're happy, whoever the hell you were.

Rackham tore himself away from the view and stumbled for the door, clutching the rum to his chest. Time to go, just like Billy had said. Let's find out if the lads had held on for their gallant leader, or if he was going down with his ship. Filled with bitterness and rum, he found he didn't care either way.

The doorway to the bridge was darkened by a figure. Good lad Billy, thought Rackham, come to collect your Captain. But the voice was not that of the young sailor.

"Going somewhere Jack?"

*

Jones stepped into the wheelhouse, keeping the pistol high and fixed on the pirate.

"You?" choked Rackham, reeling, eyes wide.

Jones nodded to the bottle in the other man's grasp. "Not sure what you're celebrating. As I climbed up here, I noticed your lads all heading south as fast as their oars would carry them. Seems you've been left behind."

Rackham adopted a sour expression, swaying on his feet, eyes blazing.

Jones kept the gun fixed on the pirate and ran his gaze over the bridge. "Nice boat. Shame she's going down."

His eyes caught on a familiar piece of equipment. There, sitting atop the ship's wireless, was a wooden box, its front panel a mass of dials, a tangle of electrical wiring sprouting from its rear. A hard knot of anger formed in his chest.

"Coded messages, eh?" he said, returning his eyes to Rackham. "You've been working for the Germans..."

"I don't work for nobody," spat the pirate. He took a swig from the bottle, spilling as much as he swallowed. "Partners, more like."

"Their spies told you which ships to attack. Targeting the cargo they didn't want to reach France."

Rackham face twisted into a sneer. "Made it sweeter – knowing I was helping kill more Englishmen."

Jones' fingers flexed on the gun. "And knowing that makes this even sweeter for me..."

"Ah, to hell with you," said Rackham. He spread his arms wide, stepping forward, bringing his chest to within inches of the muzzle of the pistol. "Do it," he said, voice flat and cold.

My pleasure, thought Jones. Like shooting a rabid dog – a kindness to everyone.

The deck pitched beneath their feet, both men stumbling as the dreadnought shifted. Jones' aim faltered as he staggered and a mad gleam sparked in Rackham's eyes.

The pirate swung his arm and the bottle smashed against Jones' skull. Glass ripped his skin and stinging liquid splashed across his eyes, sending him rearing back, his free hand flying to his face. Before he could recover his stance, Rackham was on him, desperate fingers scrabbling at the gun.

Already off-balance, and reeling from the blow to his head, he fell backwards. The pirate crashed down on top, driving Jones' breath out of him and sending a flare of agony surging up from his damaged ribs. Caught in a blaze of pain, unable to summon any strength, the pistol was wrenched from his grasp and sent tumbling away over the deck.

He felt Rackham's hands close about his throat, the pirate pressing down on him, breath hot on his face. Jones clawed at the hands around his neck. He got hold around a single finger and hauled it outwards, the bone giving way with a sharp crack. A fierce glee overcame the pain from his side as the pirate howled and rolled clear. You already tried to strangle me once Jack, he thought, sucking in great gulps of air.

Rackham rose unsteadily and lurched for the door, abandoning the fight, clutching his injured hand and cursing. Jones reached up for the rail and pulled himself to his feet. Bent almost double over his aching ribs, blind in one eye through a combination of dripping blood and cheap rum, he glowered after the retreating pirate.

"No you bloody don't."

He threw himself after Rackham, smashing into his back. They burst through the doorway, careening across the wing of the bridge. Locked together, they crashed into the rail and tipped over the edge.

The planks of the lower deck came rushing up towards them and everything went black.

*

Jones was shaken into befuddled consciousness as hands gripped his shirt and hauled him up.

His returning awareness was accompanied by a flood of pain. The broken ribs he could endure, almost accustomed to their grumbles, but entirely new hurts now clamoured for attention from across his body. He almost blacked out again as he put weight on his left foot, streaks of agony shooting up from his ankle. But unconscious twice in one day was quite enough. He concentrated, swaying, but managing to stay upright.

"Easy there Major..."

Jones cracked an eye open, wincing as the sunlight sent spots swirling across his vision. He mustered his scattered wits and Kowalski's face swam slowly into focus.

"You're alive..."

"Heh. A sight more than you by the looks of it." The Floridian regarded the bridge above them. "Still, you're in better shape than I expected after your tumble. Reckoned I was coming aboard to sweep up the pieces and take 'em back to Isabella for a keepsake."

Jones ignored the jibe, mention of the fall sparking recollection of his struggle in the wheelhouse.

"Where's Rackham?"

"You must have hit your head harder than I thought. Where's Rackham? Damned if you ain't been sleeping on him..." He gestured and Jones hobbled round to look.

Calico Jack Rackham, King of the Tortuga Pirates, lay on the sloping deck, head askew, blank eyes staring up into the cloudless sky.

"Broke your fall..." said Kowalski. "And his neck."

Their contemplation of the dead pirate was interrupted by a surge of water as the dreadnought shuddered, slipping further into the sea. The wave's backwash sucked at Rackham's corpse, dragging it forward down the deck.

Fully half the warship's length was beneath the surface. Disturbed by air escaping from the wreckage, water now boiled above the tangled steel of the collision point where Jones had clambered between the vessels. The *Great Eastern* herself was settling low, bows submerged, her paddles finally motionless. Like the dreadnought, her stern was pushed upwards as she sank at the bow, raising the blazing superstructure of her wheelhouse like some sacrificial offering. The flames roared up, belching thick black smoke into the air.

Kowalski followed Jones' gaze. "I'd never have found you without the smoke. My little boat couldn't keep up with Rackham when he tore off after you."

Jones turned from the stricken merchant ship. "Little boat?"

Kowalski waved towards the side rail. "Right this way Major. Although you may have to swim some. I didn't dare tie her to any of this mess."

Jones flexed his ankle, sucking his teeth at the stabbing pain the movement caused. "I fear I'll be more floating than swimming. I may require a tow."

Kowalski stepped close, offering his support. Together they shuffled towards the side, Jones practically carried by his companion.

"Typical top brass," muttered Kowalski. "Always leaving the lower ranks to do the heavy lifting."

At the rail, Jones turned for a last look at the carnage he had created.

Rackham's body was floating now, sloshing about amongst the debris, just one more piece of flotsam as the hungry waves devoured the ship.

*

Kowalski dragged the Englishman up from the water, hauling him over the launch's stern rail. The pair slumped to the deck, a stain of seawater spreading out from their sodden clothes, darkening the planks.

Jones was pale and drawn, clearly struggling with his various injuries. Kowalski winced in sympathy. Whilst he felt pretty beaten-up himself, the Englishman was in a whole other class of hurt – dog-tired and broken.

He clambered to his feet. "The Commodore's bound to have some liquor stashed somewhere. You look like you could use a drink."

This drew a weak smile from Jones. "I could at that." He turned his head, taking in the launch. "I thought I recognised her. Nice boat."

"It seemed a criminal waste to leave her tied up in Cayona," said Kowalski, shouting over his shoulder from the wheelhouse. "And her crew proved none too keen to die repelling boarders." He pulled a whisky bottle from a storage locker, waving it in triumph as he returned with it to the Englishman.

Jones eyed the label. "Proper Scotch," he grunted. "Bloody luxury." He pulled the cork from the neck with his teeth and spat it over the side, then lifted the bottle and took a deep swallow. He leaned his head back. "God, but that's better."

Jones handed the bottle up and Kowalski swigged from it himself. The spirit burned his throat, the warming tingle spreading down and out through his core. He looked at the label.

"I'll have to find out where Culpepper gets his booze," he said. "This stuff is good."

"Talking of the Commodore, how did our would-be President feel about losing his pretty little boat?"

Kowalski moved across to the narrow steps leading up to the wheelhouse. He couldn't help but smile as he reached for the locker door flanking the stairs.

"Why don't you ask him?"

He turned the handle and the man stuffed inside the locker's confines popped outwards, his rotund hog-tied frame thumping to the deck. Piggy eyes glared out above the rope gag that reduced Culpepper's anger to a series of muffled grunts.

Jones goggled at the sudden appearance of the American. He stared at the captive open-mouthed before recovering himself and looking up to Kowalski, face full of questions.

"Heh. Wireless started squawking as I was fixing to leave. Our friend here wanted collecting from Rackham's ship. I figured I'd oblige." Kowalski nudged the trussed man with his foot. "He didn't pay a blind bit of notice as to who might be at the wheel. Too busy getting his fat behind down the rope ladder. Damn near pooped his britches when I said hello." The expression on the American's face had been beautiful – a memory Kowalski would treasure to the end of his days. "Since then, he's been packed away in his compartment there. I reckoned you might want to discuss some things with him. Assuming you were still alive and all."

Jones pulled himself up, clutching the rail as he hobbled over to the steps. He lowered himself on to the bottom rung and stretched his injured leg out before him.

"You reckoned correctly. Untie him."

Kowalski handed his pistol over and Jones covered the captive whilst Kowalski loosened the ropes. Able to move, Culpepper manoeuvred his bulk into a sitting position against the stern rail and pulled the gag from his mouth. He worked his jaw, jowls wobbling, pink tongue flicking out to moisten cracked lips. The eyes darted from Jones to Kowalski and then back again.

"Perhaps..." he said. "Ah, perhaps we can come to an arrangement?"

Jones said nothing and Culpepper flinched from his silent regard, fixing his gaze on Kowalski instead.

"Name your price Captain..."

"It ain't that easy. Us mercenary types are choosy about who we work for."

Jones spoke, iron in his voice. "You're a disgrace Commodore. A stain on the honour of your country and your service." His face twisted. "You disgust me."

Culpepper swallowed. "The degenerates will find their supply, whoever delivers it. All I was doing –"

"This isn't about your drug-running," interrupted Jones. "And it's not about your deal with Rackham." He paused, eyes downcast, staring at the deck for an age before lifting his gaze, focused once more. "It's not even about my brother."

The pistol came up, the weapon rock-steady in the Englishman's grip. "This is about the villagers you've been terrorising for months. The people you were supposed to protect."

Culpepper's lip curled beneath his whiskers. "And for those peasants you'll appoint yourself judge and jury?"

The gun roared in Jones' hand.

The American clutched his leg and howled. Jones struggled to his feet, staring down at the injured man. Culpepper quailed before the look, screams fading into strangled sobs as blood seeped up between his fingers from the ruined meat of his thigh.

"I'll cheerfully stand judge and jury over the likes of you," said Jones. "However I draw the line at executioner. Instead, I'm going to give you the same chance your pirate friends gave all those British sailors." He turned a stone cold gaze to Kowalski. "Throw him over the side."

Culpepper's keening returned at full pitch. "No!" he screeched. "The blood... the sharks..."

Jones turned his back on the injured American, plucked the whisky bottle from Kowalski's grip, and shuffled up the steps into the wheelhouse.

Kowalski reached down and grabbed Culpepper's lapels. The man sobbed, pleading, podgy fingers pawing at him. Kowalski hauled him upright and stared into the flushed, sweating face.

"You picked a fight with the wrong man there Commodore..."

He gave the American a shove.

Culpepper's mouth gaped wide as he toppled backwards over the rail. He struck the water with an almighty splash, disappearing beneath the waves before struggling upwards, arms flailing.

The boat's engine rumbled into life, prompting renewed howls from the man in the water, incoherent calls interrupted by frequent dips under the surface. The launch steamed away from the sinking ships and the floundering American, Culpepper's desperate pleas echoing inside Kowalski's head long after they had faded from his hearing.

*

Havana

Jones lifted a hand, shading his eyes to follow the course of a fat airship as it passed across the bay, heading for the docks.

He raised his teacup and took a sip, pleased at the lack of trembling clatter as he returned the cup to its saucer – a definite improvement from the previous day. However, the motion did prompt grumbles from the ribs beneath the tight bandages and, not to be outdone, the dull throb from his ankle flared up. He ignored both complaints and closed his eyes, soaking up rays of the morning sun.

The peace was interrupted by Kowalski, bursting through the doors and out onto the balcony. "Have you seen the papers?"

Jones nodded, tapping a finger on the stack of folded publications beside his breakfast tray. *Navy Hero Lost Defending English Ship From Pirates* proclaimed the headline on the topmost page.

The periodicals beneath all recounted similar stories, and had done for days – ever since the news had made it over the straits to the American mainland. The only aspect of the tale to vie with Culpepper's passing for top billing had been the arrival in Havana's harbour of the wounded *Neptune*, the great Brunel at the helm, towing a flotilla of lifeboats laden with survivors.

"Unbelievable," said Kowalski. "Next thing they'll be trying to canonise the bastard."

"The authorities know the truth. Let Culpepper enjoy his posthumous glory." Jones adjusted the cushion beneath his raised foot. "How are the negotiations proceeding?"

Kowalski snorted. "A damned talking shop is all they are. Nobody willing to quit yapping long enough to hear what the other side is saying."

"Better than the alternative..."

The American administration, embarrassed by the revelations of Culpepper's activities had reluctantly entered into discussions with Estrada and his insurgents. The Floridians were moderating the talks and Kowalski had been pressed into service monitoring security.

"Nearly forgot. I picked something up for you..."

Kowalski fished a small wooden box from his pocket and deposited it on the table, nodding to Jones to open it.

Inside, nestled on a bed of dark blue velvet, shone the brushed metallic casing of a pocket watch. Jones lifted it out, thumbing the catch to reveal a mechanical marvel – an intricate mechanism of cogs, springs and levers gleaming beneath the crystal glass of the watch's open face.

"As promised," said Kowalski. "Ramon assured me it was a good one."

"I don't know what to say..."

Kowalski got to his feet. "Then don't say anything." He waved a hand towards Jones' injured ankle. "You can buy me a drink when you're up and about."

Jones returned the Floridian's smile. "I might even buy you two."

"Heh. I'll see you around Major."

Kowalski departed, leaving Jones running his fingers over the smooth matte surface of the watch. His reverie was broken by Isabella's arrival. She bent over him and pressed her lips to his own, her black curls tumbling across his face. She pulled away, beaming down at him.

"And how is my patient this morning?"

"Better. And better still if more of that treatment is forthcoming."

Her eyes sparkled. "Perhaps. But we must be careful. You are an invalid after all." She settled herself in her seat, slipping her fingers beneath the silk at the top of her dress to withdraw an envelope. "More correspondence from the telegraph office. You are a popular man."

The past three days had seen an endless procession of visitors traipsing through the Mirador to speak with Jones. Most – like the Americans or the British Consul – to discuss the political ramifications of the events on Tortuga. Others – like Brunel and Turner – more interested in the progress of Jones' recuperation. The whole period had been punctuated with regular telegraph messages from London – a mixture of congratulations for a job well done, or admonishment for the cost to the Treasury of scuttling the *Great Eastern*.

Isabella handed the envelope across. The paper was still warm from contact with her skin. Jones slid his finger beneath the flap, opening the fold and pulling out the card.

Return at earliest opportunity. Still a war on. – B

He stared down at the printed words.

"What is it?" asked Isabella.

Jones lifted his gaze to the woman across the table, regarding her for as long as he had stared at the telegram.

She gave an uncertain smile under his scrutiny, fingers twisting at a strand of hair.

He folded the message card over on itself and tore it into two neat halves. He stacked the pieces and tore them through again before depositing the resulting scraps amidst the remains of his breakfast.

Leaning back in his chair, Jones clicked open the pocket watch and peered at the mechanism, the tiny gears spinning as the second hand ticked its way round the dial.

"Nothing," he said, returning his attention to Isabella. "Nothing that can't wait a while."

*

Acknowledgements

If you've made it this far, here's a huge thank you from me. I genuinely appreciate you giving the book a go and I really hope you've enjoyed it.

I would love to hear what you thought of it, either in reviews on Amazon or Goodreads, or you can contact me more directly at: www.redmercuryblogspot.co.uk

Once again a whole bunch of people encouraged and supported me whilst I tried to get this thing written. Particular thanks go out to:

- Judy and Toby for a fantastic stay in their lovely house 'Lochside', where the first outline was written
- The brave Beta Readers who ploughed their way through early drafts, pointing out gaping plot holes and picking up the typos. The best bits of the book are undoubtedly down to the suggestions they made. The worst bits remain all my own. Cheers to Richard, Chris, Alex, Aidan, Doug, Suzanne and Thanuja
- Al, scary editor-in-chief and source of the single best plot suggestion EVER
- Danny and Blythe for putting up with dad tapping at his laptop every evening for months

Most of all, thanks to everyone who took a chance on *Red Mercury* and were kind enough to tell me it wasn't awful. This one is your fault.

Printed in Great Britain
by Amazon.co.uk, Ltd.,
Marston Gate.